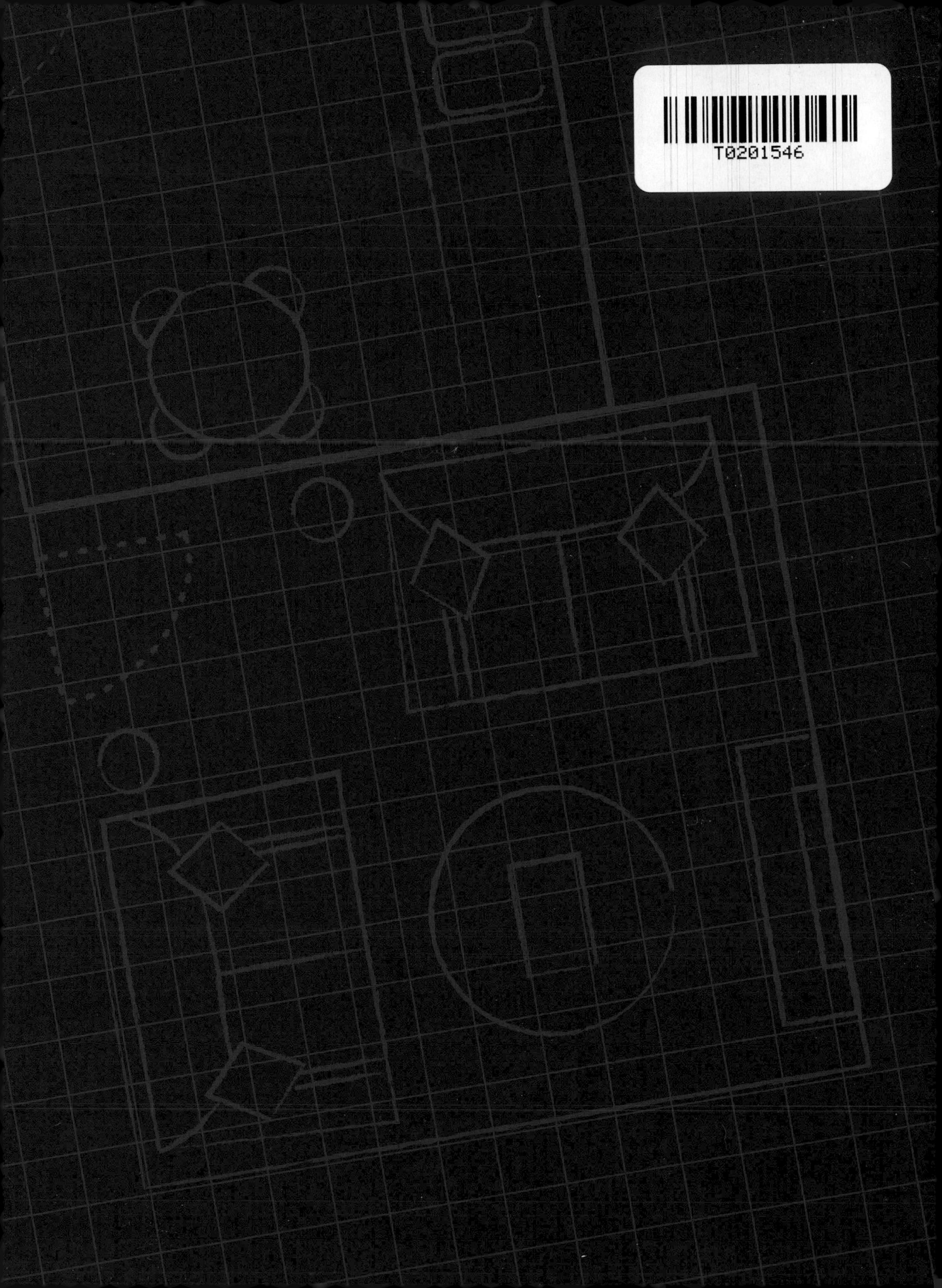
T0201546

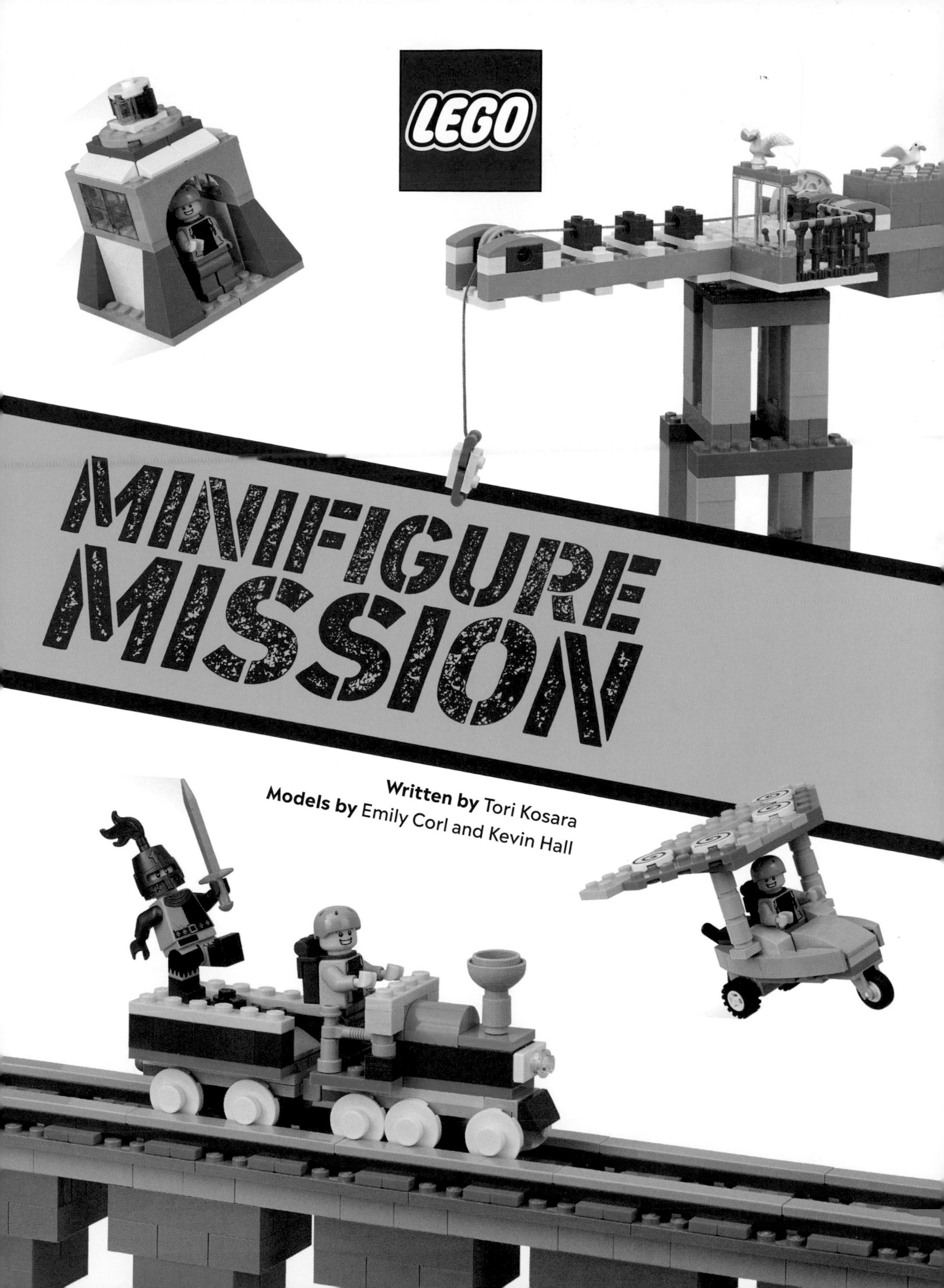

LEGO MINIFIGURE MISSION

Written by Tori Kosara
Models by Emily Corl and Kevin Hall

CONTENTS

I'M READY TO ROLL!

SPECIAL MISSION

A minifigure is in trouble! He has been left in the bathroom and needs to get back to his friends on the toy shelf. Use your LEGO® collection and your building skills to help him navigate around pesky pirates, dodge dirty dust bunnies, escape from the vacuum cleaner, and much more. Will he make it home safely?

BIG CHALLENGE

It's a long way from the bathroom to the toy shelf. Plus there are a lot of obstacles along the way. It will take skill for this minifigure to build his way home. He can definitely use your help.

A PLACE OF YOUR OWN

Homes come in all shapes and sizes with different features and types of furniture. If the place you live doesn't have a bathtub, for example, think about how you could build your way across a shower stall instead. There is no limit when it comes to your imagination!

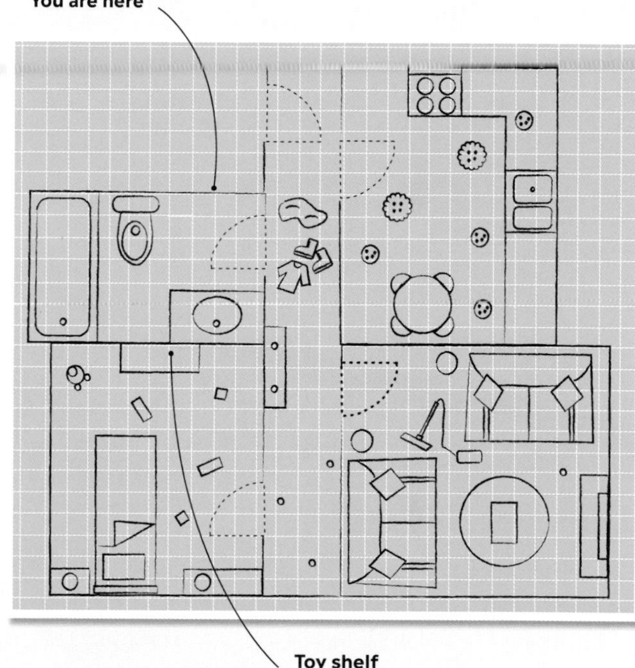
You are here
Toy shelf

PREPARE FOR YOUR MISSION

Here are some handy tips for building your way through any LEGO mission.

USE YOUR IMAGINATION

If you don't have a particular piece, think about other elements you can use instead.

ORGANIZE YOUR BRICKS

Sort your collection by colors and types before you build. This will save time when you start building.

DON'T WORRY!

If your model doesn't turn out the way you wanted, start again or change it into something else. The most important part of the mission is to have fun!

MEET CHARLIE

Charlie has been left on the windowsill in the bathroom by mistake. His mission is to make it back to the safety of the toy shelf. He'll need some special equipment and plenty of help with ideas and building to get there.

Safety gear like this helmet protects Charlie during his mission
I'M READY FOR THIS MISSION!
Comfortable clothing is great for running, jumping, and climbing

MISSION EQUIPMENT

Every adventurer needs the right tools. Charlie has some handy gear in his rucksack to help him on his journey.

Pickax for climbing
Large rucksack holds gear
Skateboard for zooming around
Flippers for swimming and sticky situations

MEET THE ADVENTURERS

A mission can be hard work, but it is much easier with friends to help! Meet some of the minifigures that help Charlie along the way. Then spot them in the adventure on the pages that follow.

ISABEL

Isabel lives on the toy shelf. She uses her own special equipment, including a walkie-talkie, to help guide Charlie on his journey home.

MAYA

This minifigure is also lost! Maya and Charlie team up to help each other get back to the toy shelf, and have lots of fun along the way.

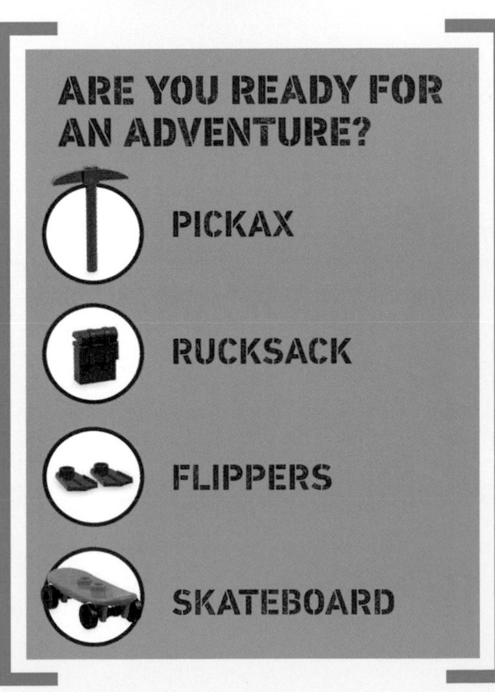
ARE YOU READY FOR AN ADVENTURE?
PICKAX
RUCKSACK
FLIPPERS
SKATEBOARD

LET'S GO!

CHAPTER 1
BATHROOM

BATHROOM
THIS LOOKS LIKE A MONSTER OF A MISSION!
IT'S A JUNGLE IN THERE!

BATHROOM
AHOY!

LOFTY LEDGE

Charlie should be on the toy shelf, not in the bathroom. It's a long way home! First, Charlie needs to get down from the windowsill, but how? Eek! A cranky jungle explorer has spotted him, so he needs to think quickly!

THE PLAN = ?

OBSTACLES

JUNGLE EXPLORER

FOREST OF HOUSEPLANTS

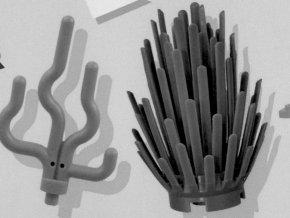

1X4 SLOPE

1X1 ROUND PLATE WITH BAR

1X2 CURVED SLOPE

1X1 BRICK

USEFUL BRICKS

JUNGLE WALKWAY

BUILDING IDEAS

AMPHIBIOUS VEHICLE

. . . THAT'S IT!

A jungle walkway will keep Charlie safely suspended over the gap between the windowsill and the sink. It's a good thing that the jungle explorer doesn't like to leave the Forest of Houseplants!

CABLES

Charlie's weight is supported by a line of cables. They attach to a platform at either side of this suspension bridge.

I HOPE I DON'T WOBBLE!

Stack bricks at angles to create a tree

1

1x2 plates form a railing

Bars and clips connect to form cables

Stack of 2x2 bricks gives the platform its height

LEAF US ALONE!

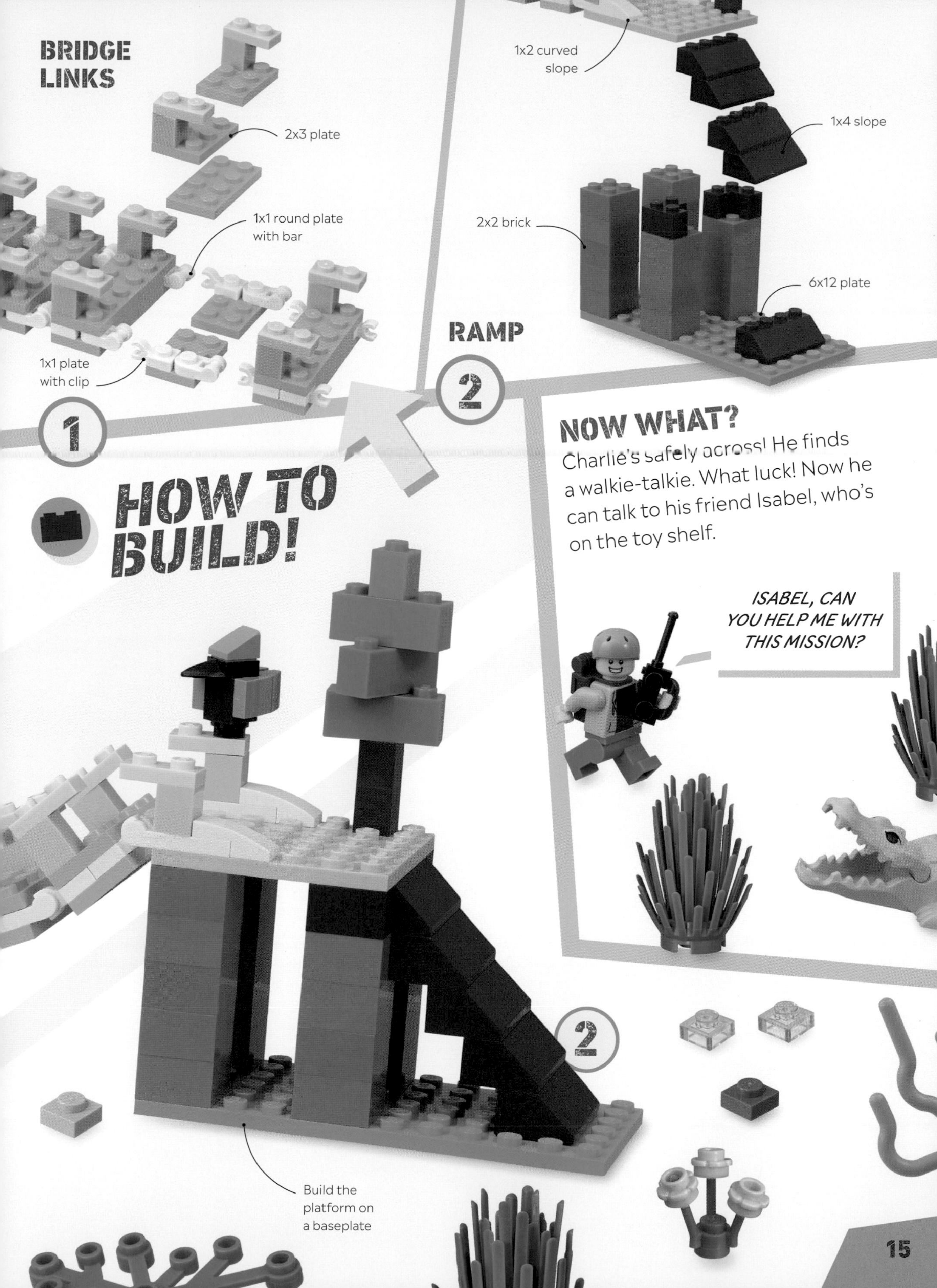
BRIDGE LINKS
2x3 plate
1x1 round plate with bar
1x1 plate with clip
1
1x2 curved slope
1x4 slope
2x2 brick
6x12 plate
RAMP
2
HOW TO BUILD!
NOW WHAT?
Charlie's safely across! He finds a walkie-talkie. What luck! Now he can talk to his friend Isabel, who's on the toy shelf.
ISABEL, CAN YOU HELP ME WITH THIS MISSION?
2
Build the platform on a baseplate

ZIPPING AWAY

Charlie's on the sink, but he's pretty far from the ground. If Charlie can get to the bathtub edge, he might be able to reach the floor. There's also the small matter of escaping from a sea monster! What should he do?

THE PLAN = ?

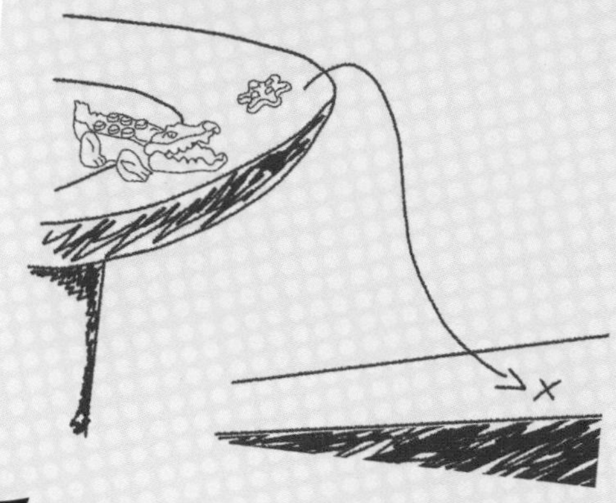

OBSTACLES

SEA MONSTER FROM THE SINK

TOOTHPASTE BLOBS

HUNGRY CROCODILES

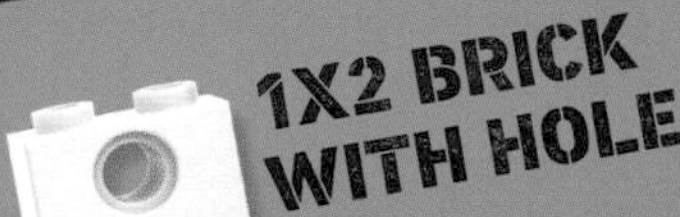
1X2 BRICK
WITH HOLE

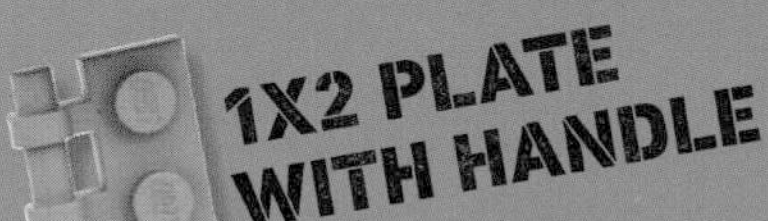
1X2 PLATE
WITH HANDLE

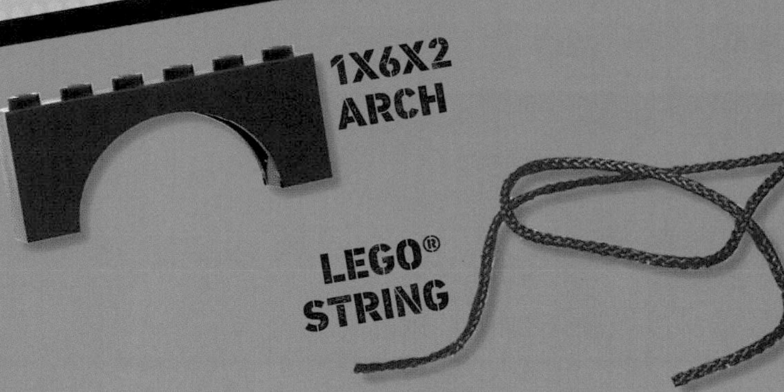
1X6X2
ARCH
LEGO®
STRING

USEFUL BRICKS

BUILDING IDEAS

ZIP LINE

DRAGONFLY TO RIDE ON

LOOK OUT FOR THOSE HUNGRY CROCS, CHARLIE!

. . . THAT'S IT!

Whee! Charlie quickly builds a zip line. Gliding across the string will keep him out of harm's way as he slides to the bathtub edge. Soon he will be one step closer to the safety of the toy shelf.

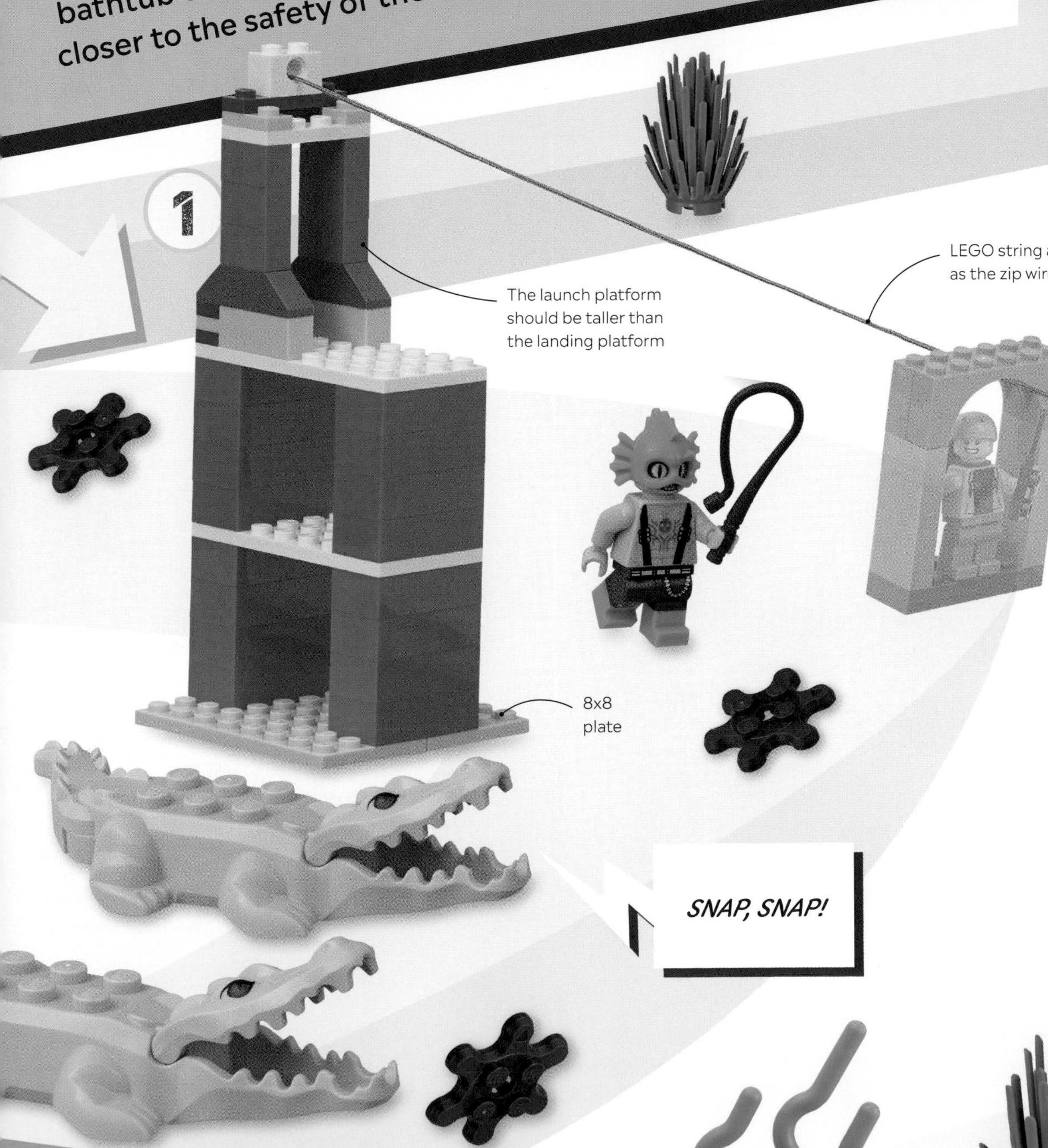
1
The launch platform should be taller than the landing platform
LEGO string acts as the zip wire
8x8 plate
SNAP, SNAP!

HOW TO BUILD!

SLOPE

Charlie can control the speed at which he slides down the zip line by changing the angle of the line. A steeper slope increases the velocity (speed)—Charlie goes faster!

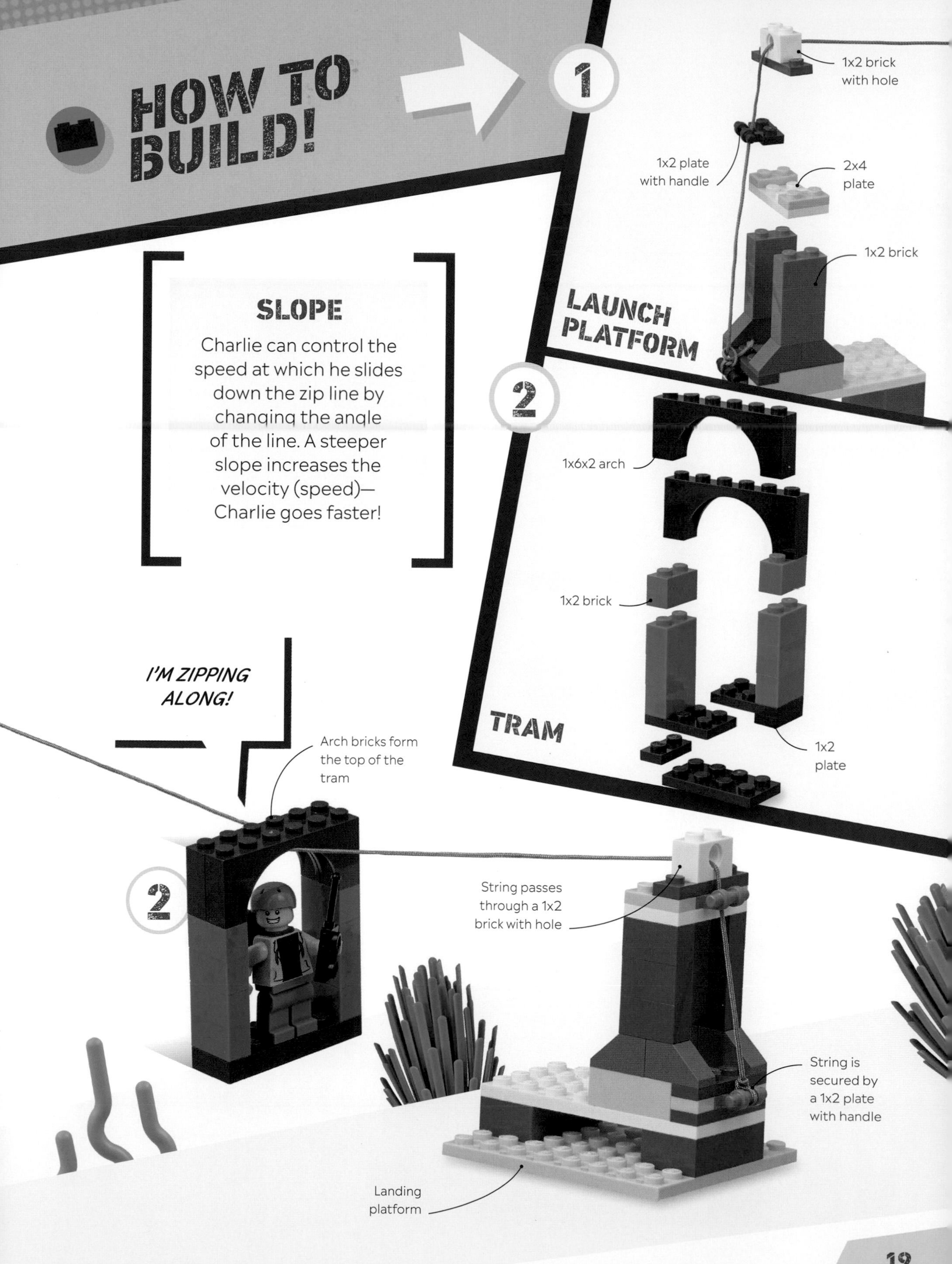

1
1x2 brick with hole
1x2 plate with handle
2x4 plate
1x2 brick
LAUNCH PLATFORM
2
1x6x2 arch
1x2 brick
1x2 plate
TRAM
I'M ZIPPING ALONG!
Arch bricks form the top of the tram
2
String passes through a 1x2 brick with hole
String is secured by a 1x2 plate with handle
Landing platform

HIGH AND DRY

Charlie lands on the bathtub's edge. He carefully walks along the narrow path. There is a tower of bubbles in his way, and there are bars of slippery soap. The only place to go is down into the empty bathtub! What should he ride?

THE PLAN = ?

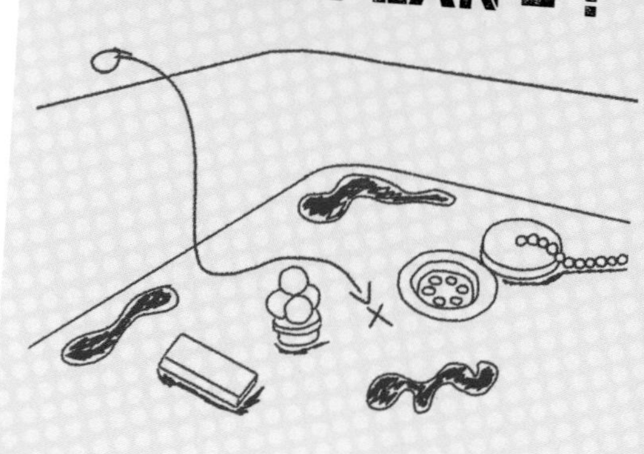

OBSTACLES

BARS OF SOAP

TOWER OF BUBBLES

I'LL JUST HOP INTO THE TUB.

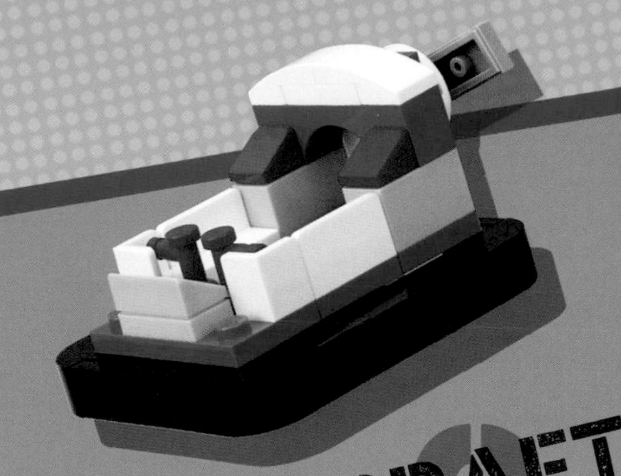

SEA PLANE

HOVERCRAFT

MONSTER TRUCK

BUILDING IDEAS

IT LOOKS LIKE YOU'LL HAVE TO GO INTO THE BATH!

USEFUL BRICKS

2X2 TURNTABLE

1X2X1⅓ CURVED BRICK

1X2 BRICK

TAP PIECE

1X2 SLOPE

. . . THAT'S IT!

Charlie makes a hovercraft and rides it into the tub. Oh no! There is a menacing looking pirate ship ahead. The amphibious vehicle, which can travel on land or through water, glides past with ease. Phew!

Make a mast using brown plates

Build ship railings with plates

AHOY! 'TIS AN UNWELCOME LANDLUBBER.

1x2 curved slope

Slope for anchor blade

Tap piece looks like vehicle controls

1x2x1⅓ curved brick forms the corner of the skirt

2

HOW TO BUILD!

1 PROPELLER

1x2/2x2 angle plate

2x2 turntable

2x2 round jumper plate

1x4 tile

AIR

There is a cushion of air between the skirt of a hovercraft and the smooth surface below it. The air carries the weight of the craft so it can glide.

2

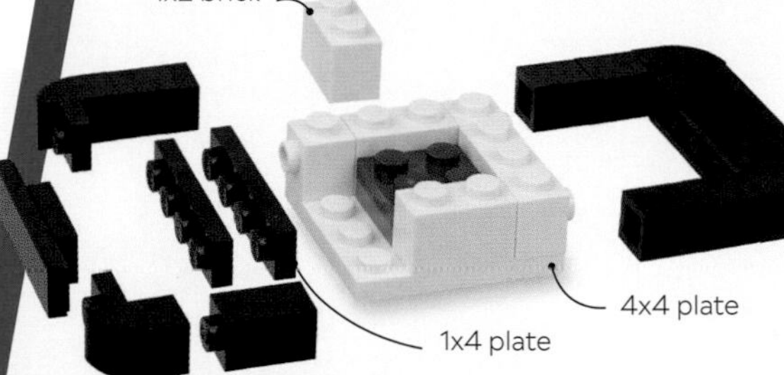

1x1 brick with side stud
1x2 brick
4x4 plate
1x4 plate
1x2x1 ⅓ curved brick

BASE

1

1x1 corner panel

Tile spins on a 2x2 turntable to make a propeller

PIRATE PROBLEM

The pirates on the ship don't seem happy that Charlie is in their tub. He had better get out of here!

SHIVER ME TIMBERS!

PERILOUS PIRATES

Pop, pop, pop! The sound of bubbles fills Charlie's ears. But he can hear something else. Oh no! It's the grumpy pirates from the ship. Charlie tries to scale the side of the bathtub, but it's too slippery. How can he get out?

THE PLAN = ?

OBSTACLES

YOU'RE IN
ARRRGH
BATHTUB!

GRUMPY PIRATES

OFF YOU GO,
MATEY!

USEFUL BRICKS

1X2 BRICK
WITH HOLE

2X6 BRICK

2X2 BRICK

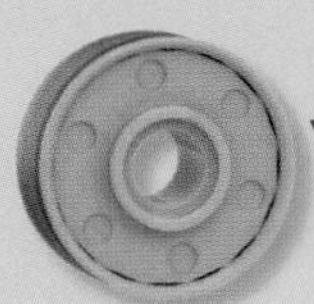

WHEEL

1X2X2
PANEL

THE ONLY WAY OUT IS UP!

BUILDING IDEAS

RESCUE HELICOPTER

PULLEY SYSTEM

. . . THAT'S IT!

Charlie designs a clever pulley system to pull himself out of the tub. The seat will lift him up and lower him down to the ground safely. Charlie hoists himself upward just before the pirate captain can grab him!

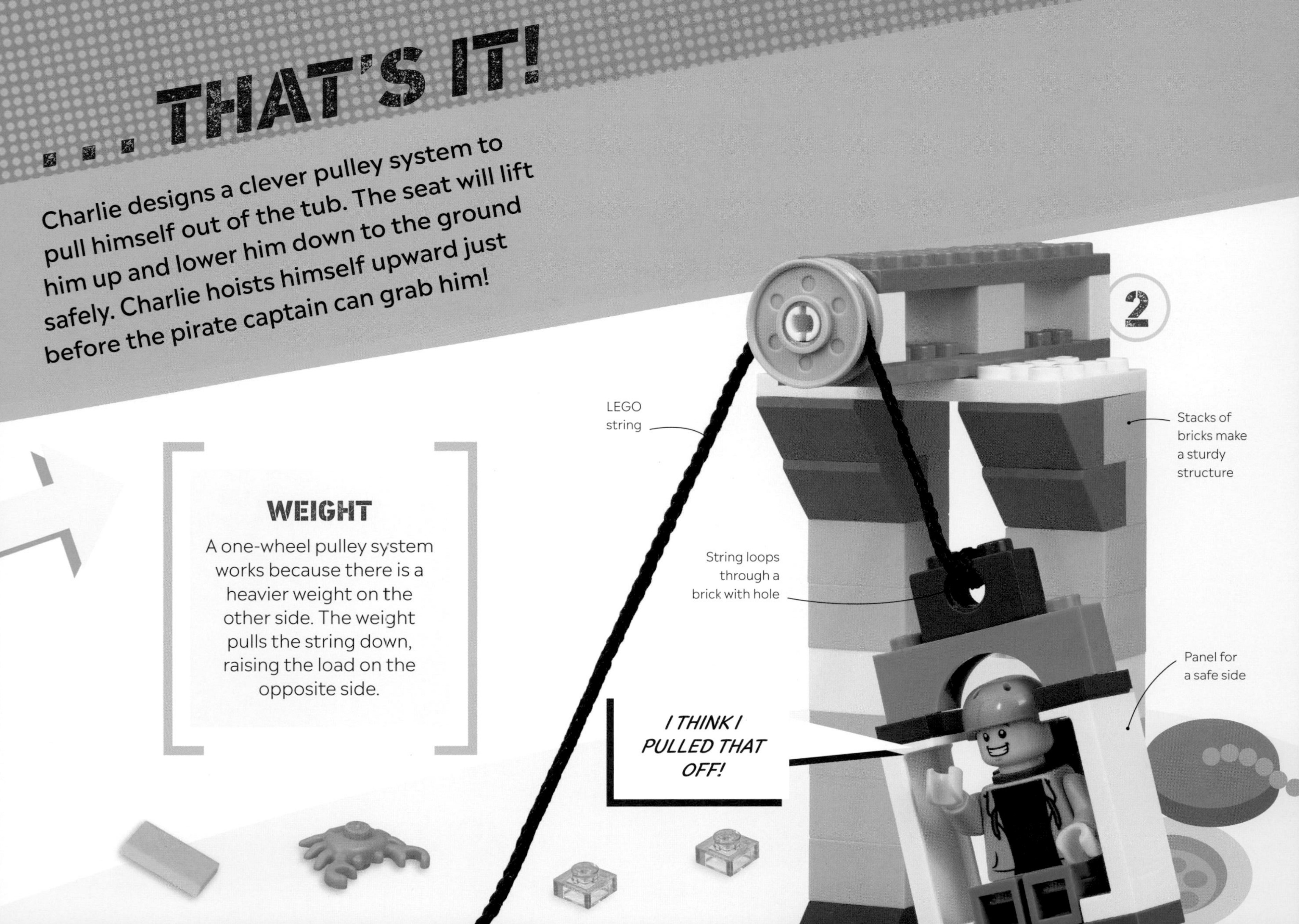
2
LEGO string
Stacks of bricks make a sturdy structure
String loops through a brick with hole
Panel for a safe side
I THINK I PULLED THAT OFF!

WEIGHT

A one-wheel pulley system works because there is a heavier weight on the other side. The weight pulls the string down, raising the load on the opposite side.

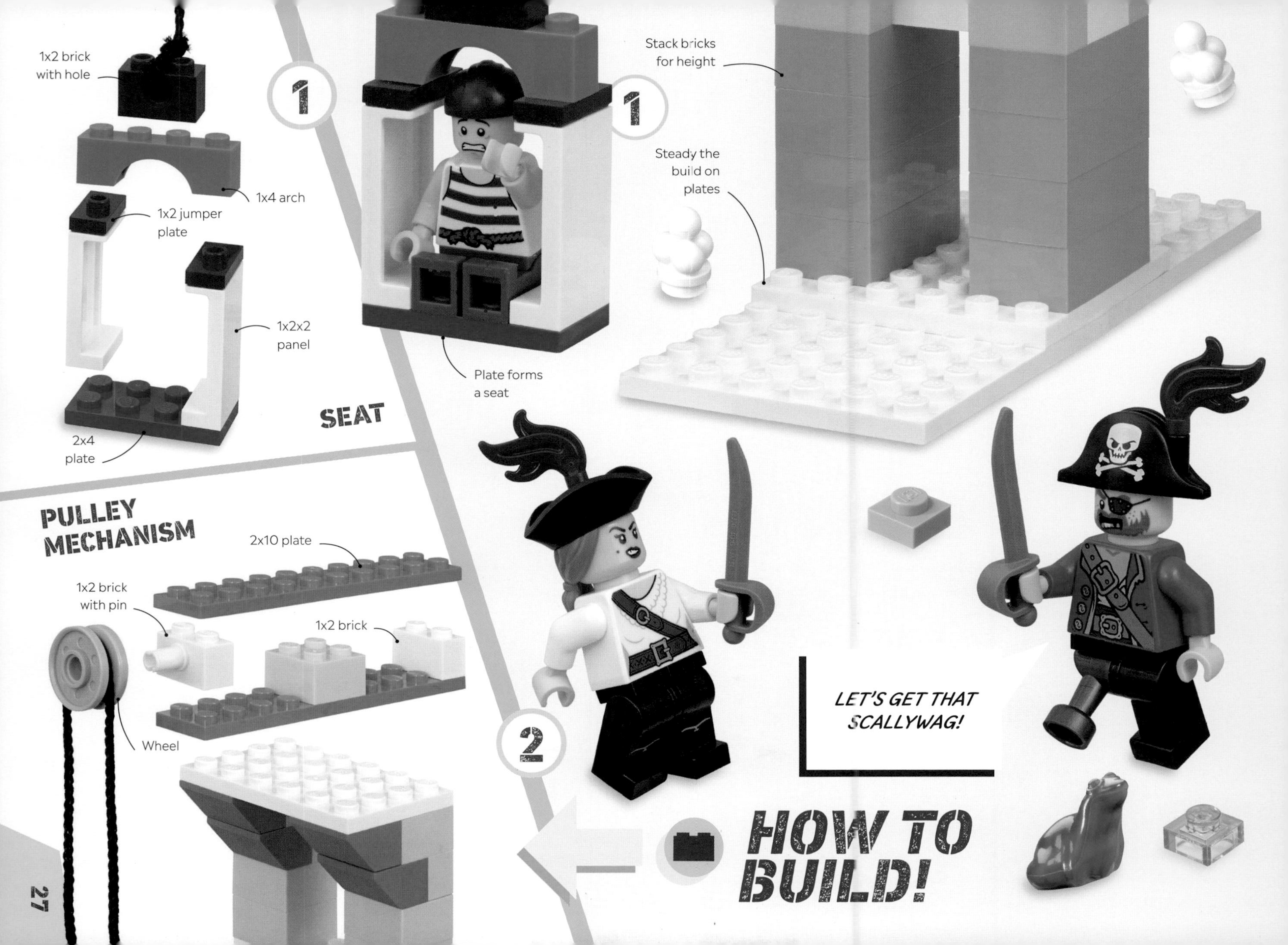
SEAT
1
1x2 brick with hole
1x4 arch
1x2 jumper plate
1x2x2 panel
2x4 plate
1
Plate forms a seat
Stack bricks for height
Steady the build on plates
PULLEY MECHANISM
2x10 plate
1x2 brick with pin
1x2 brick
Wheel
2
LET'S GET THAT SCALLYWAG!
HOW TO BUILD!

UP AND AWAY!

The pulley system topples over as Charlie climbs out. The pirates can't scale the tub's smooth sides, but—*bump*! Charlie knocks into a rubber duck and ruffles his grouchy feathers. Charlie needs to get up to the doorknob and out of here!

THE PLAN = ?

OBSTACLES

BAD-TEMPERED RUBBER DUCK

JUMPY FROG

GRUMPY PIRATES

FIRE ENGINE LADDER

CABLE CAR

BUILDING IDEAS

CATAPULT

QUICK! THOSE PIRATES ARE NOT HAPPY.

USEFUL BRICKS

1X2 PANEL

1X2 BRICK WITH PIN

2X4 PLATE

4X4 ROUND RING PLATE

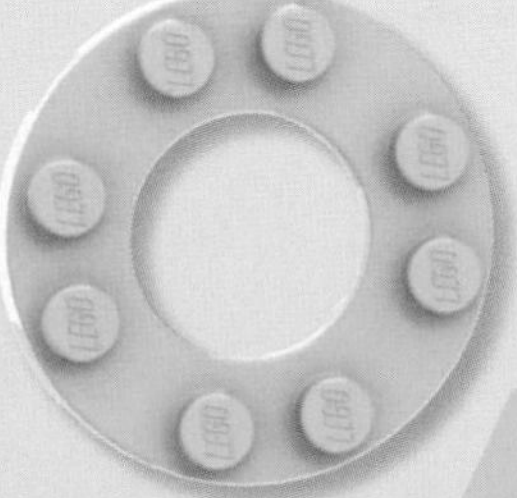

. . . THAT'S IT!

Charlie makes a catapult. It will launch him through the air and up to the doorknob. But how can he get it to work? Aha! The jumpy frog is hopping his way. The frog leaps onto the opposite side of the catapult and Charlie flies up to the doorknob!

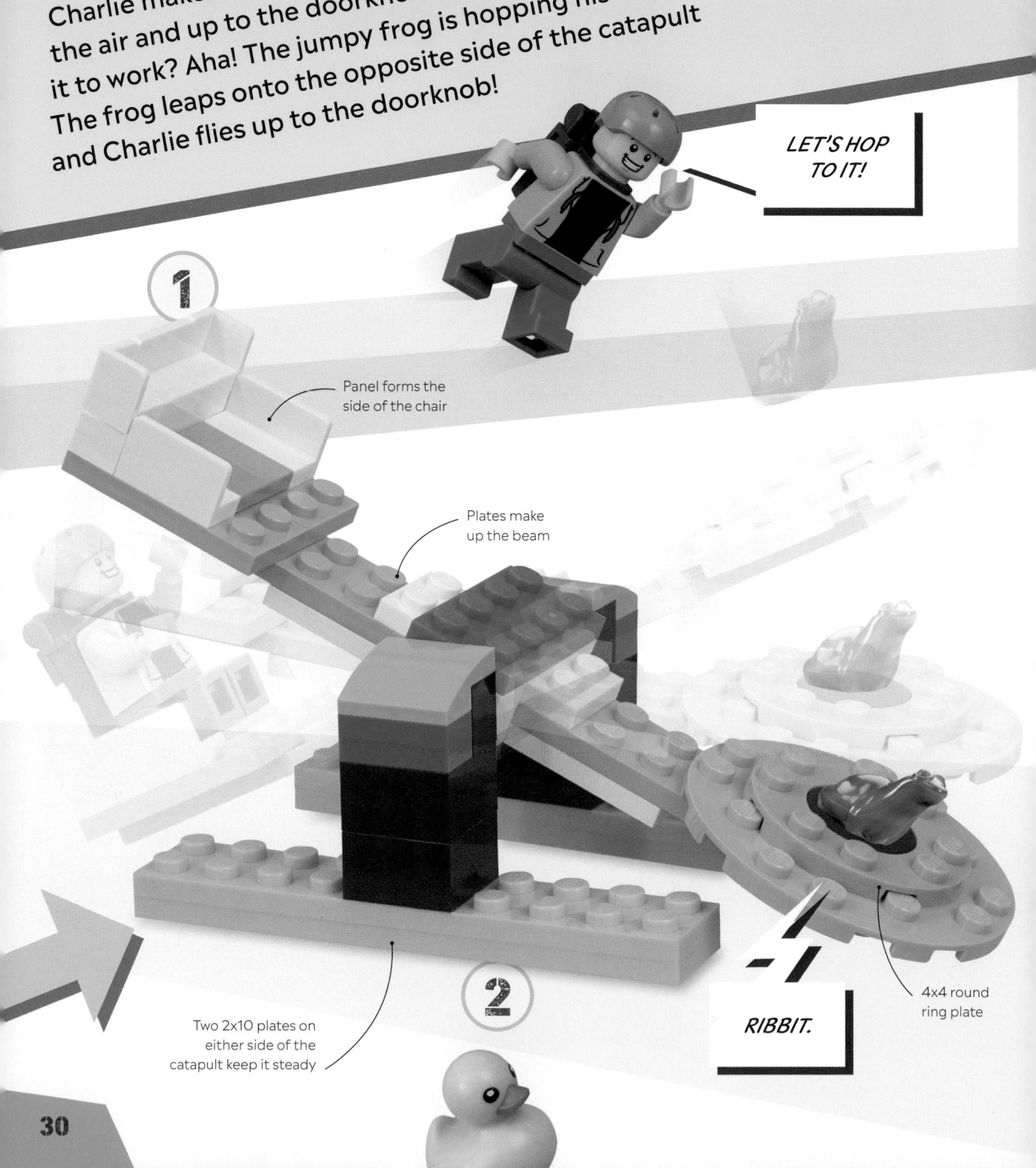

LET'S HOP TO IT!
1
Panel forms the side of the chair
Plates make up the beam
2
Two 2x10 plates on either side of the catapult keep it steady
RIBBIT.
4x4 round ring plate

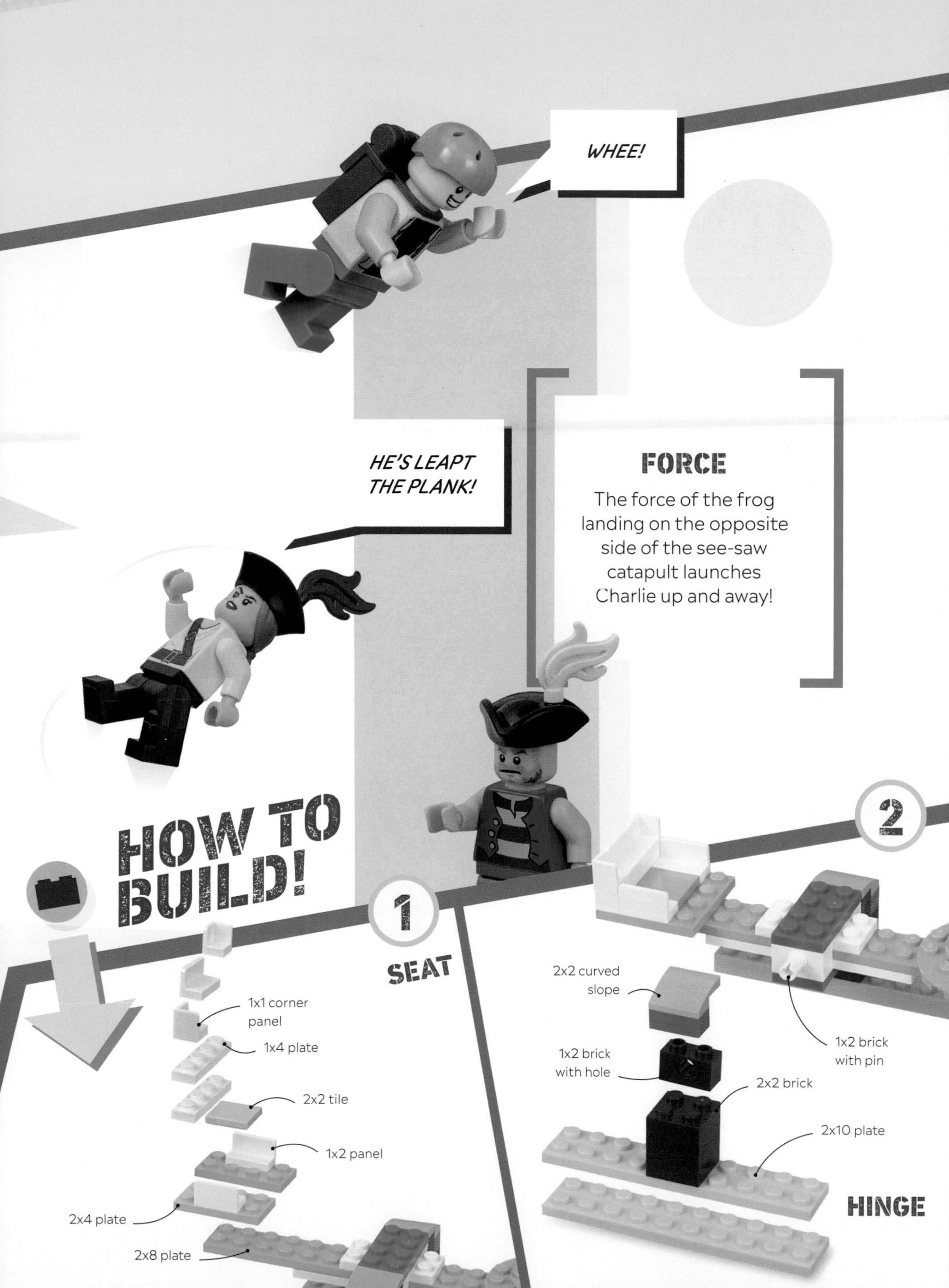
WHEE!
HE'S LEAPT THE PLANK!
FORCE
The force of the frog landing on the opposite side of the see-saw catapult launches Charlie up and away!
HOW TO BUILD!
1
SEAT
1x1 corner panel
1x4 plate
2x2 tile
1x2 panel
2x4 plate
2x8 plate
2
2x2 curved slope
1x2 brick with hole
2x2 brick
2x10 plate
1x2 brick with pin
HINGE

CHAPTER 2
HALLWAY

IT'S A SKELE-TON OF FUN IN THIS CORRIDOR!
WELCOME TO THE HAUNTED HALLWAY.

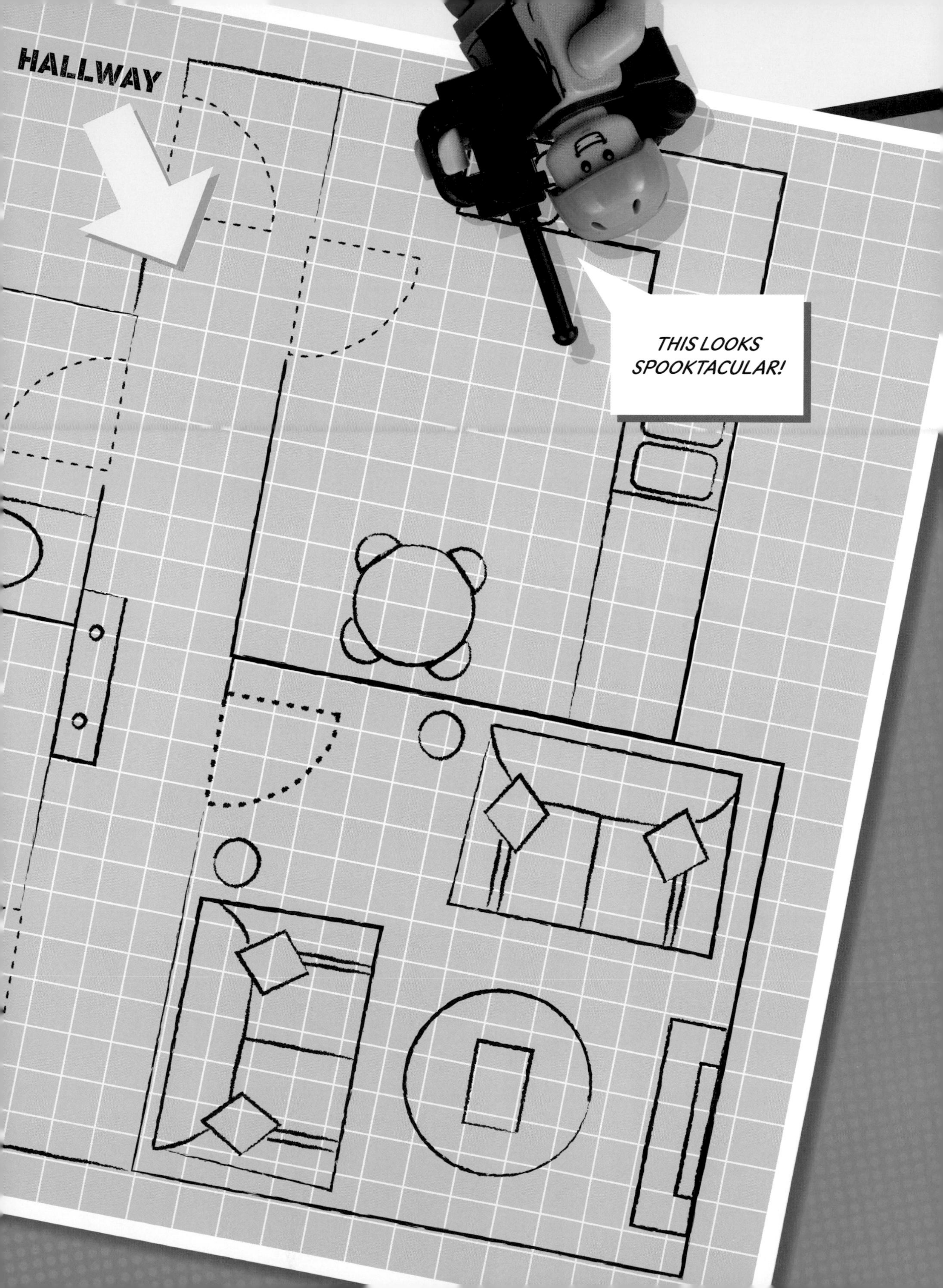
HALLWAY
THIS LOOKS SPOOKTACULAR!

WING IT!

Charlie is well on his way back to the toy shelf now. He has made it to the hallway but he needs to get off of this doorknob, and fast! This is a perch for eagles and Charlie is not welcome up here. How can he get down?

THE PLAN = ?

BUILDING IDEAS

CHAIN OF LINKS TO CLIMB

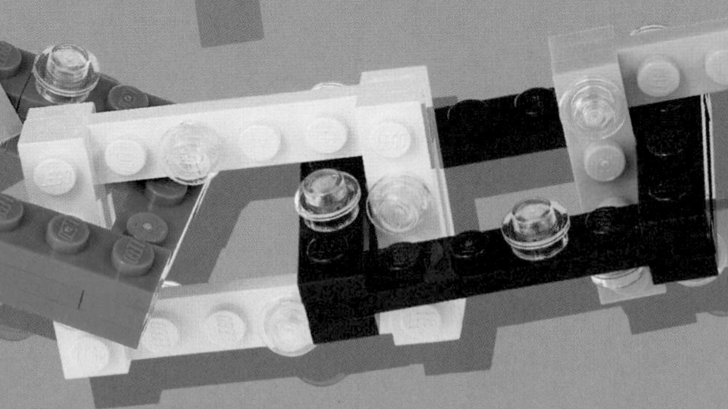

OBSTACLES

TIME TO FLY, CHARLIE!

UPSET EAGLES

ULTRALIGHT

USEFUL BRICKS

2X2 PLATE WITH PINS

2X2 PLATE WITH WHEEL BEARING

PROPELLER

2X3 WEDGE PLATE

. . . THAT'S IT!

An ultralight is just what Charlie needs. With this amazing aircraft, he can sail off of the bathroom doorknob. Ready, set, go! Charlie climbs aboard and flies away from the angry eagles.

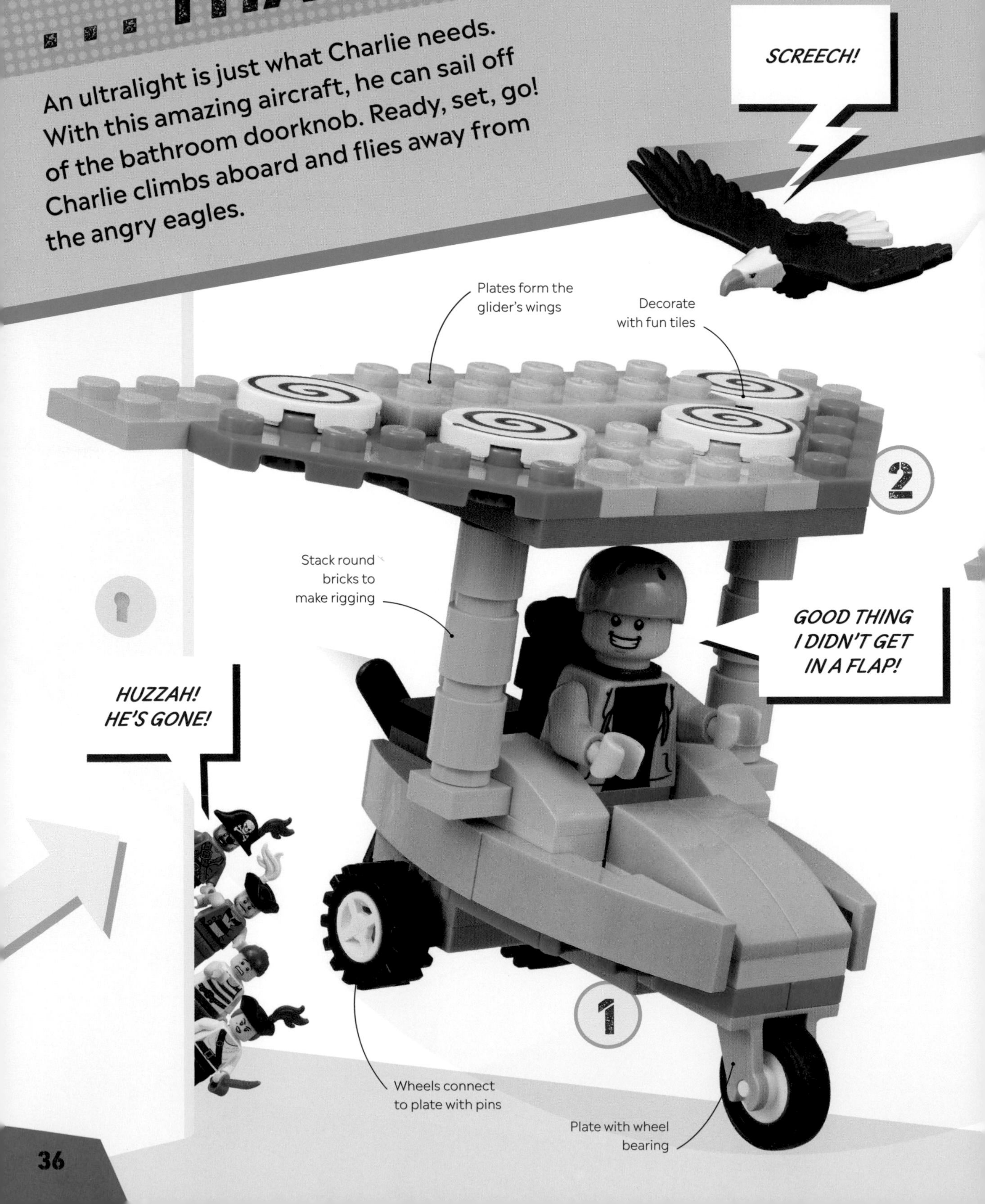

SCREECH!
Plates form the glider's wings
Decorate with fun tiles
2
Stack round bricks to make rigging
GOOD THING I DIDN'T GET IN A FLAP!
HUZZAH! HE'S GONE!
1
Wheels connect to plate with pins
Plate with wheel bearing

HOW TO BUILD!

1

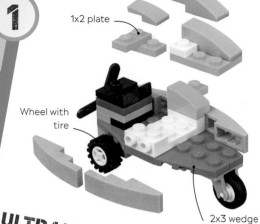

1x2 plate
Wheel with tire
2x3 wedge plate

ULTRALIGHT BODY

2

2x2 round printed tile

6x6 plate
2x6 plate

WING

WINGSPAN

An ultralight is a type of glider. It has broad wings that catch currents of rising air beneath them. The currents keep the vehicle gliding in the air.

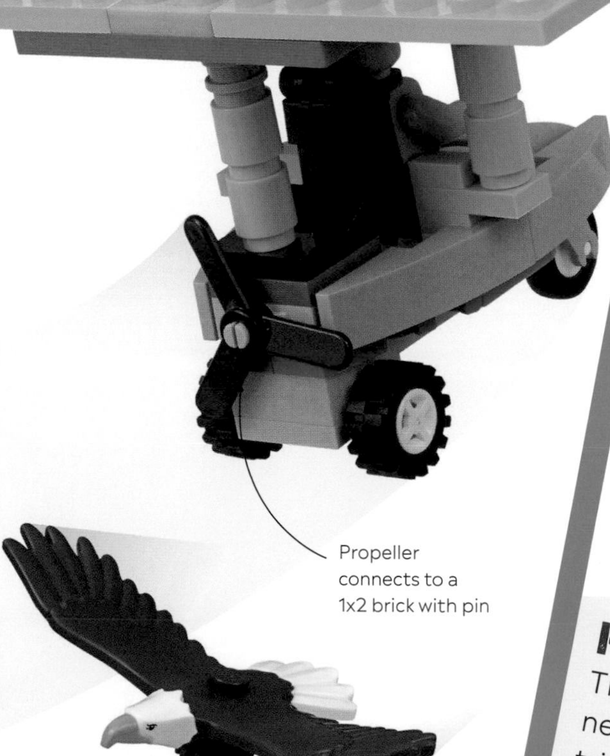

Propeller connects to a 1x2 brick with pin

ROCKY RIDE

The breeze from a nearby fan makes it too tricky for Charlie to stay airborne for long . . .

IN A SPIN

It's hard landing the ultralight among the clutter of the corridor. Charlie makes his way over piles of things on the floor, but he has an uneasy feeling. Is he being followed? Yikes! He needs to get away from these monsters!

THE PLAN = ?

OBSTACLES

SPOOKY MONSTERS

PILES OF JUNK

THIS IS A MONSTROUS CHALLENGE.

USEFUL BRICKS

2X10 PLATE

SMALL WHEEL

1X3 CURVED SLOPE

2X2 BRICK

1X3X2 INVERTED ARCH

CURVED PLATE WITH HOLE

BUILDING IDEAS

ALIEN DISGUISE

ROLLER COASTER

. . . THAT'S IT!

The best way out of this haunted hallway is on a roller coaster. Everyone knows that spooky creatures dislike being dizzy. Charlie straps in and zooms away from the clutches of the ghoulish gang.

HOW TO BUILD!

Curved arch bricks create a hill

THIS IS SCARILY FUN!

1

THAT THING IS MAKING ME DIZZY!

I HAVE A BONE TO PICK WITH THIS INTRUDER!

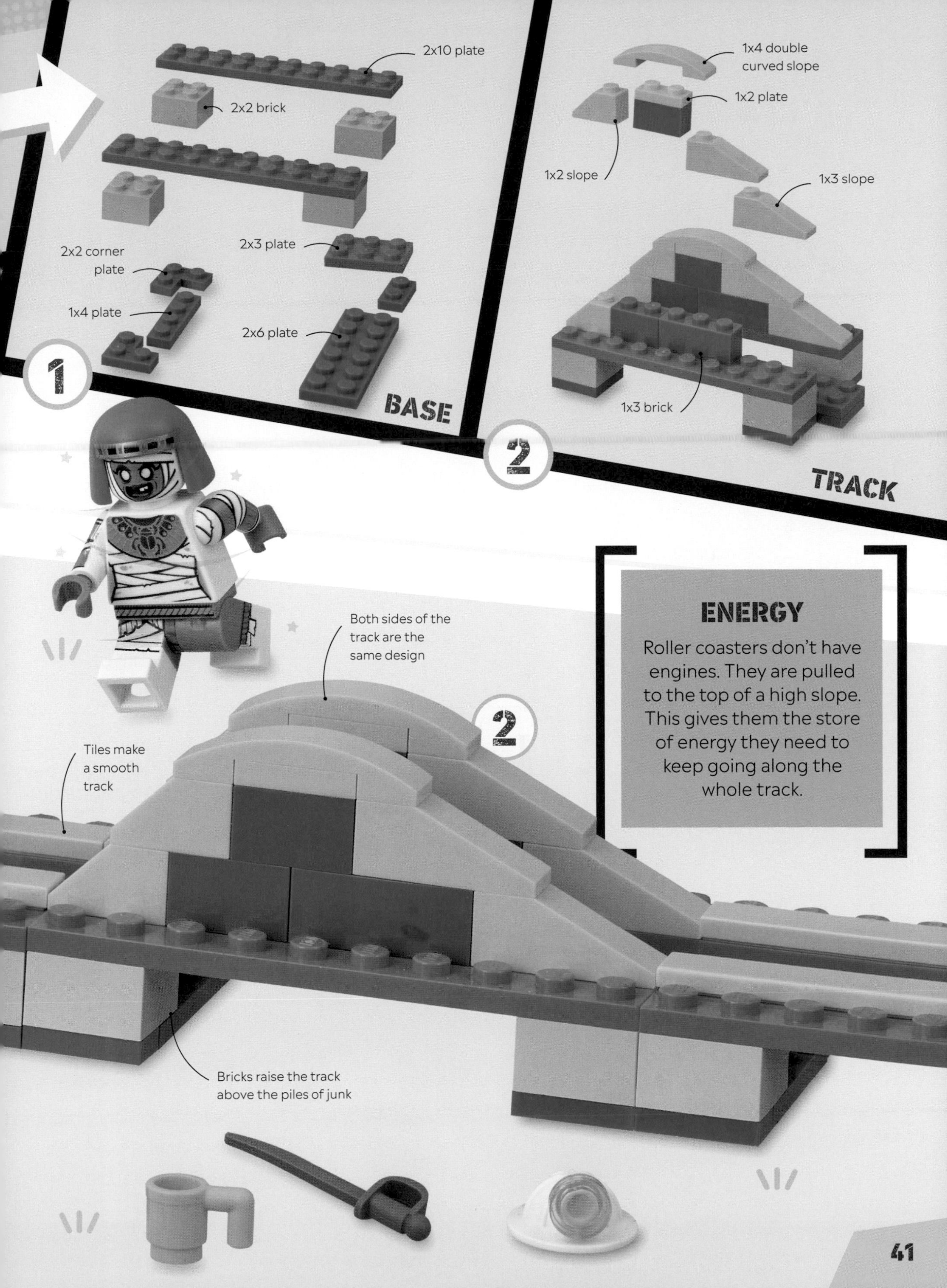
2x10 plate
2x2 brick
2x2 corner plate
2x3 plate
1x4 plate
2x6 plate
1
BASE
1x4 double curved slope
1x2 plate
1x2 slope
1x3 slope
1x3 brick
2
TRACK
Both sides of the track are the same design
2
Tiles make a smooth track
Bricks raise the track above the piles of junk

ENERGY

Roller coasters don't have engines. They are pulled to the top of a high slope. This gives them the store of energy they need to keep going along the whole track.

ROLL ON . . .

I DON'T FEEL VERY WELL . . .

A ROLLER COASTER IS A FRIGHTFULLY GOOD IDEA.

Roller coaster car has a safety bar

1

HOW TO BUILD!

THE VAMPIRE LOOKS LIKE HE'S SEEN A GHOST.

BRAKES

Roller coaster cars use brakes to stop. When engaged, brakes rub the wheels and create a force called friction. This force slows the roller coaster down.

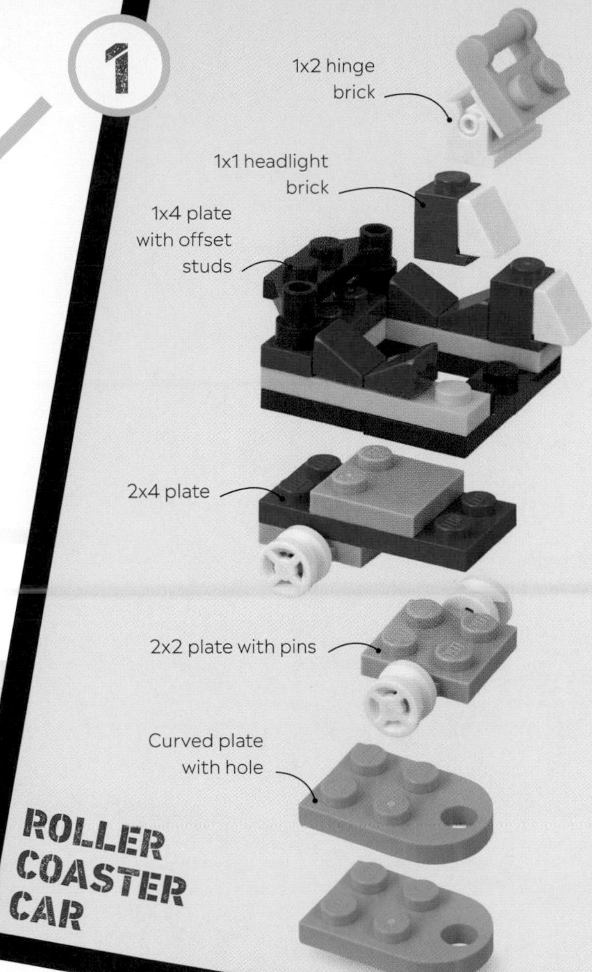
1
1x2 hinge brick
1x1 headlight brick
1x4 plate with offset studs
2x4 plate
2x2 plate with pins
Curved plate with hole

ROLLER COASTER CAR

END OF THE LINE

Charlie hops out of the car. He runs from the dizzy monsters, but something blocks his way.

CARRIED AWAY

Charlie stands in front of a mountain of boots and coats. The monsters are a bit dizzy from watching the roller coaster, but they are coming out of their daze. Charlie needs to get over this huge hill quickly! But how?

THE PLAN = ?

USEFUL BRICKS

1X2 BRICK WITH HOLE

2X2 BRICK

1X4 DOUBLE CURVED SLOPE

LEGO® TECHNIC AXLE

DUNE BUGGY

BUILDING IDEAS

OBSTACLES

LARGE ICICLES

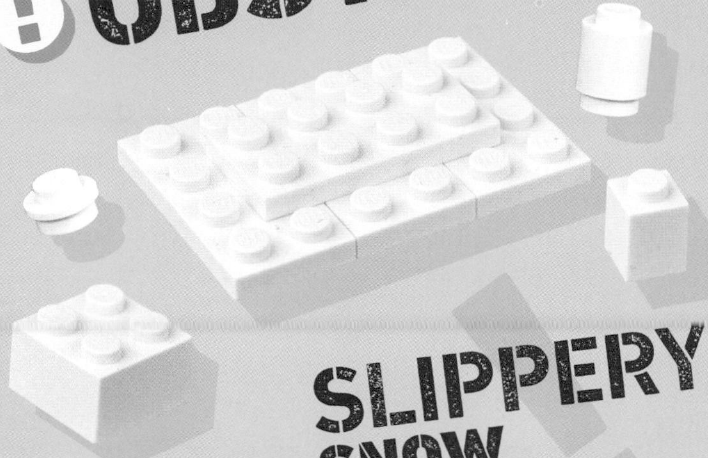

SLIPPERY SNOW

DIZZY MONSTERS

CRANE

THE MONSTERS ARE GAINING ON YOU!

PICKAX

. . . THAT'S IT!

Charlie builds a crane, but who can operate it? There is a builder doing road work nearby! Charlie asks for help and the builder climbs into the crane's cab. The crane hoists Charlie up to the peak of the mountain.

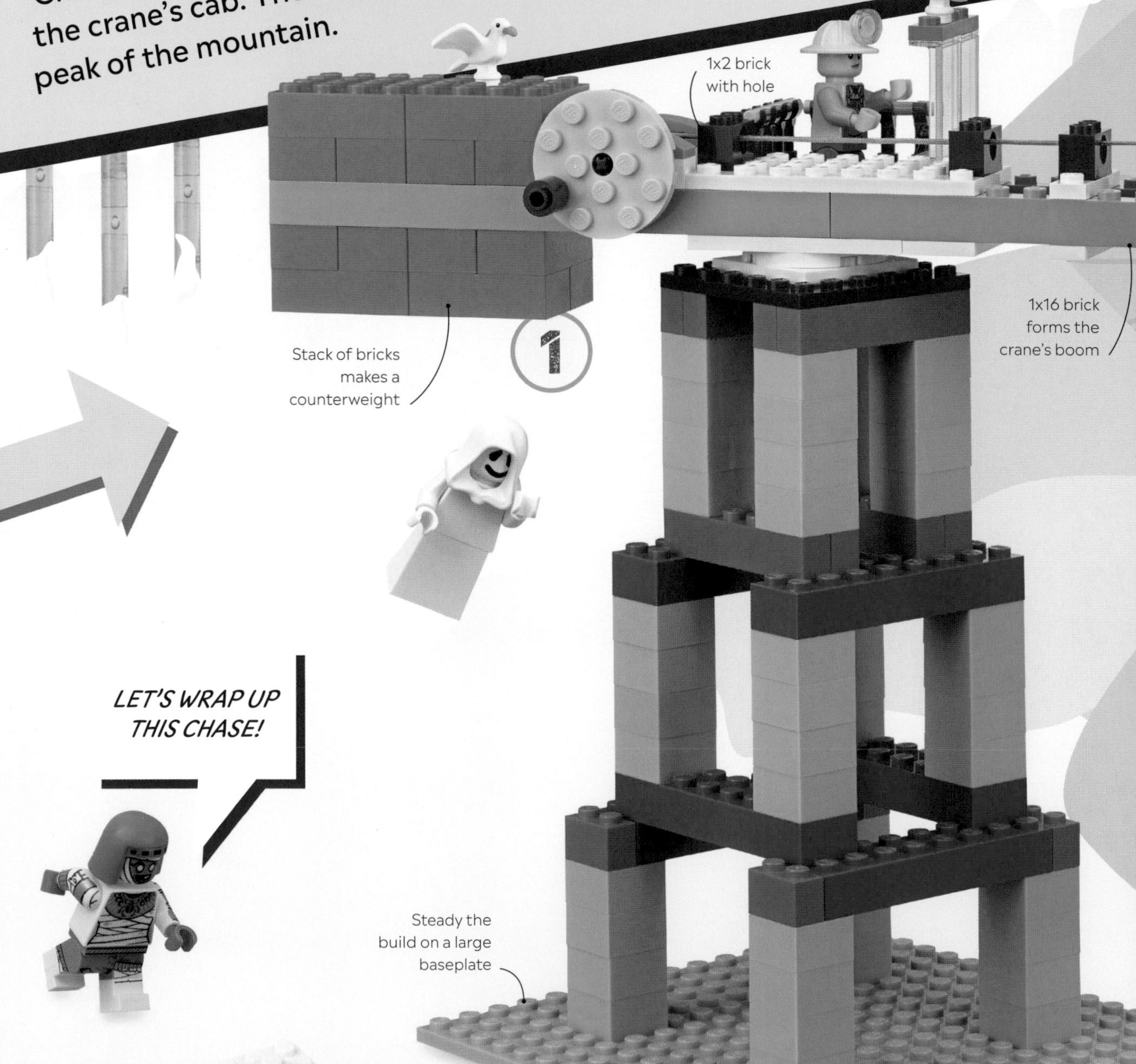
1x2 brick
with hole
1x16 brick
forms the
crane's boom
Stack of bricks
makes a
counterweight
1
LET'S WRAP UP
THIS CHASE!
Steady the
build on a large
baseplate

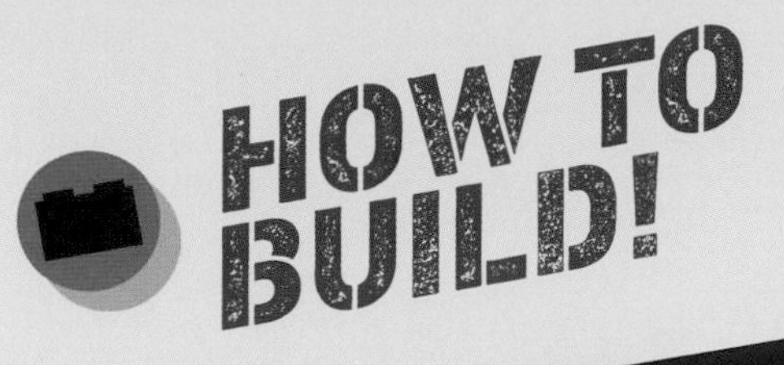

HOW TO BUILD!

1 HANDLE

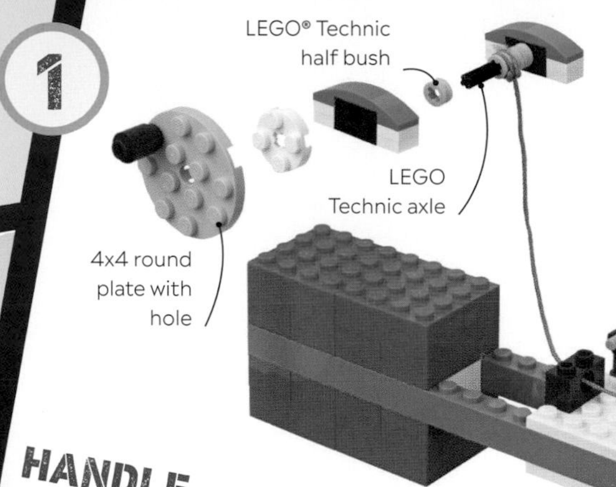

LEGO® Technic half bush
LEGO Technic axle
4x4 round plate with hole

2 PULLEY

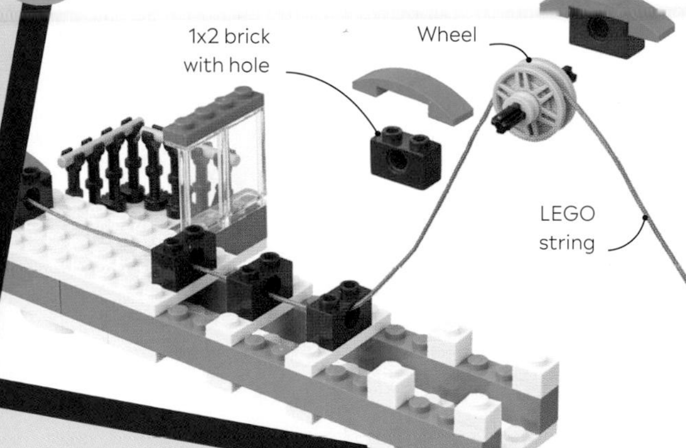

1x2 brick with hole
Wheel
LEGO string

COUNTERWEIGHT

Why doesn't this tower crane topple over when it lifts Charlie? The stack of orange bricks behind the cab is heavy enough to balance the machine so that it doesn't fall.

2

Add a cable with LEGO string

1x1 plate with bar

NEED A LIFT?

I CAN'T BEAR TO LOOK BEHIND ME!

OVER AND OUT

Charlie is on top of the mountain and there is a polar bear behind him. He needs to get down from here quickly!

SLIP OR SLIDE

Charlie can see the kitchen! He's closer to home, but he freezes in his tracks. There's a frosty snow queen who does not like visitors and a polar bear is chasing him. How will Charlie get away and go down the steep mound?

THE PLAN = ?

OBSTACLES

UNFRIENDLY SNOW QUEEN

PILES OF SNOW

POLAR BEAR

1X4 SLOPE

1X2 BRICK

1X2 PLATE WITH BAR

LADDER WITH CLIPS

1X4X2 BAR WITH STUDS

LOOK OUT, CHARLIE!

USEFUL BRICKS

BUILDING IDEAS

SKATE RAMP

SNOWMOBILE

. . . THAT'S IT!

With his skateboard at the ready, Charlie quickly builds a skate ramp so he can whiz past the snow queen and the polar bear. Charlie zooms down the skate ramp and rolls across the floor. That was close!

1
Guard rail
FREEZE, INTRUDER!
Ladder with clips
Stack up bricks for height
Slope bricks create a smooth ramp
2
GRR!

HOW TO BUILD!

1 LADDER

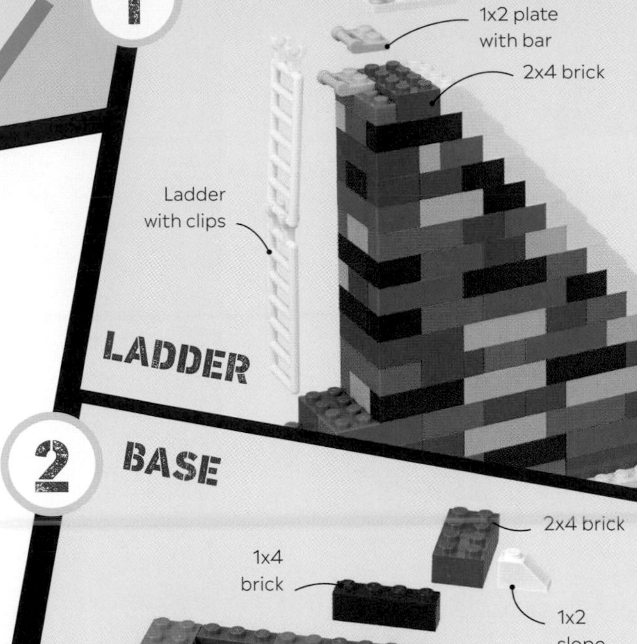
1x4x2 bar with studs
1x2 plate with bar
2x4 brick
Ladder with clips

2 BASE

2x4 brick
1x4 brick
1x2 slope

FRICTION

Friction is an invisible force that slows objects by pulling in the opposite direction. Smooth things like the ramp and wheels have little friction. They slip past each other to send Charlie zooming.

THERE'S "SNOW" WAY YOU'LL CATCH ME!

ROLL ON!

Woohoo! Charlie glides into the kitchen on his skateboard. He's getting closer to home!

THAT WAS AN "ICE" ESCAPE!

CHAPTER 3
KITCHEN
MAYBE I'LL FIND
A NICE SNACK
IN HERE!
I MUST DEFEND
THE ROUND
KITCHEN TABLE!

KITCHEN
YOU'RE ENTERING THE KITCHEN!

FLYING START

Charlie hops off his skateboard. He tries to dodge some cookies and crumbs on the kitchen floor. Suddenly, a group of rats scurries toward him. They don't want anyone touching their goodies! How can he get away?

THE PLAN = ?

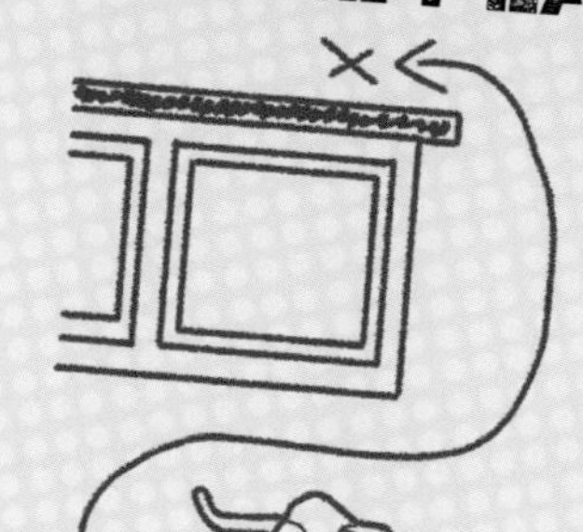

OBSTACLES

COOKIES AND CRUMBS

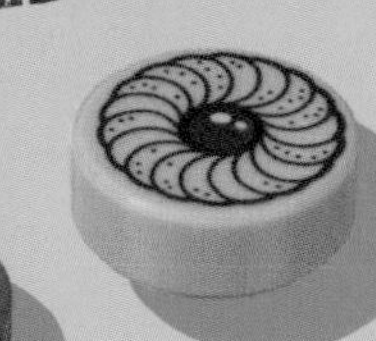

PACK OF RATS

OH RATS!

USEFUL BRICKS

2X2 TRANSPARENT SLOPE

CUPCAKE PIECE

2X3 SLOPE

1X1 ROUND BRICK

1X1 HEADLIGHT BRICK

I THINK IT'S BEST TO FLY OUT OF HERE, CHARLIE!

BUILDING IDEAS

BLIMP

AIRPLANE

. . . THAT'S IT!

An airplane will fly Charlie up and over the crumbs and rats. He hops into the cockpit and takes off into the air. Maybe he will be able to zoom all the way back to the toy shelf in this amazing aircraft!

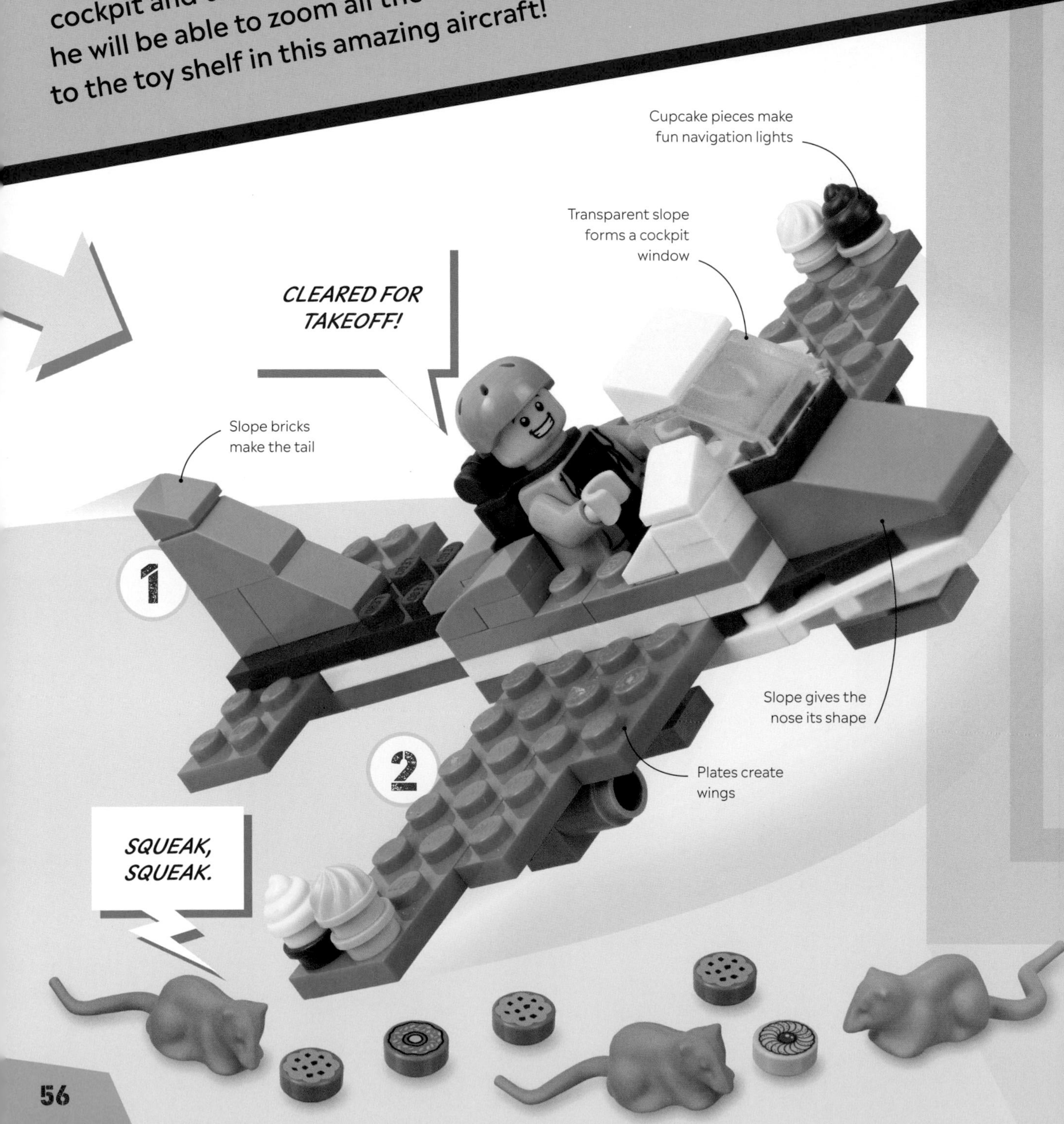
Cupcake pieces make fun navigation lights
Transparent slope forms a cockpit window
CLEARED FOR TAKEOFF!
Slope bricks make the tail
1
2
Slope gives the nose its shape
Plates create wings
SQUEAK, SQUEAK.

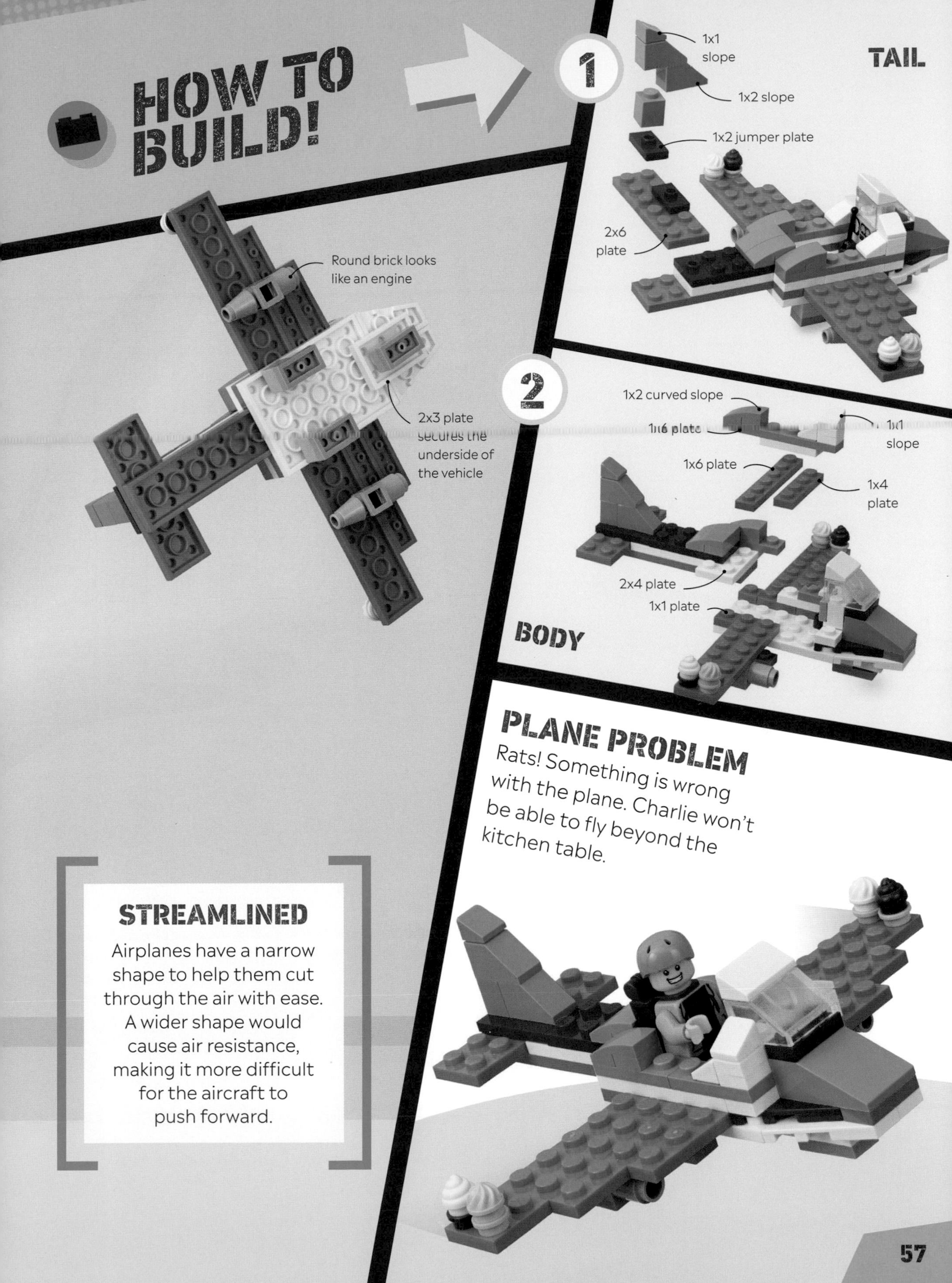

HOW TO BUILD!

Round brick looks like an engine
2x3 plate secures the underside of the vehicle
1
TAIL
1x1 slope
1x2 slope
1x2 jumper plate
2x6 plate
2
1x2 curved slope
1x6 plate
1x1 slope
1x6 plate
1x4 plate
2x4 plate
1x1 plate
BODY

PLANE PROBLEM

Rats! Something is wrong with the plane. Charlie won't be able to fly beyond the kitchen table.

STREAMLINED

Airplanes have a narrow shape to help them cut through the air with ease. A wider shape would cause air resistance, making it more difficult for the aircraft to push forward.

MAKE TRACKS

Charlie manages to make a smooth landing on the kitchen table. Suddenly, Charlie realizes that he's being followed by the Knights of the Round Kitchen Table . . . and they do not welcome guests! What should he do?

THE PLAN = ?

OBSTACLES

POOLS OF STICKY JAM

UNFRIENDLY KNIGHTS

HEY! THIS IS OUR KITCHEN TABLE.

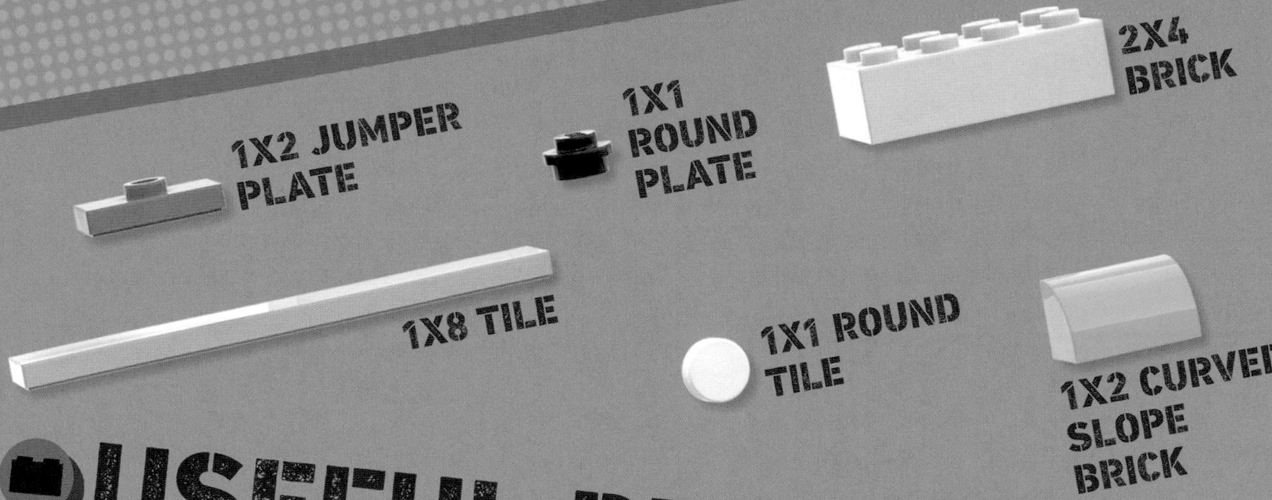

1X2 JUMPER PLATE

1X1 ROUND PLATE

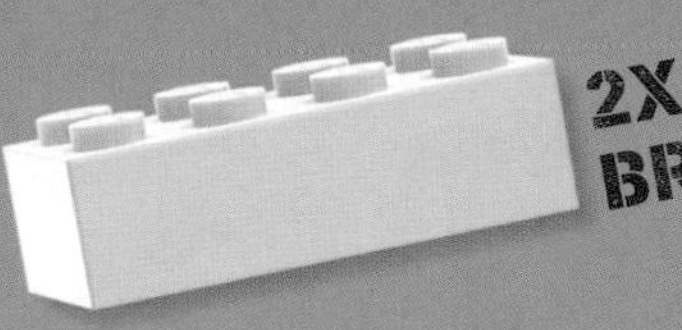

2X4 BRICK

1X8 TILE

1X1 ROUND TILE

1X2 CURVED SLOPE BRICK

USEFUL BRICKS

STONE FORTRESS TO HIDE IN

BUILDING IDEAS

ELEVATED TRAIN

. . . THAT'S IT!

Charlie cleverly builds an elevated train to get him closer to the counter. He hops into the engine car, but a knight grabs onto the coal tender. Charlie chugs on until he reaches the end of the track and the table.

IT'S THE END OF THE LINE FOR YOU!

Inverted dome for a chimney

1

Stud rests on the rail made of tiles

I WASN'T TRAINED TO RUN THIS FAR!

Stacks of bricks make sturdy supports

Use small or large plates to help the build stand up

HOW TO BUILD!

1

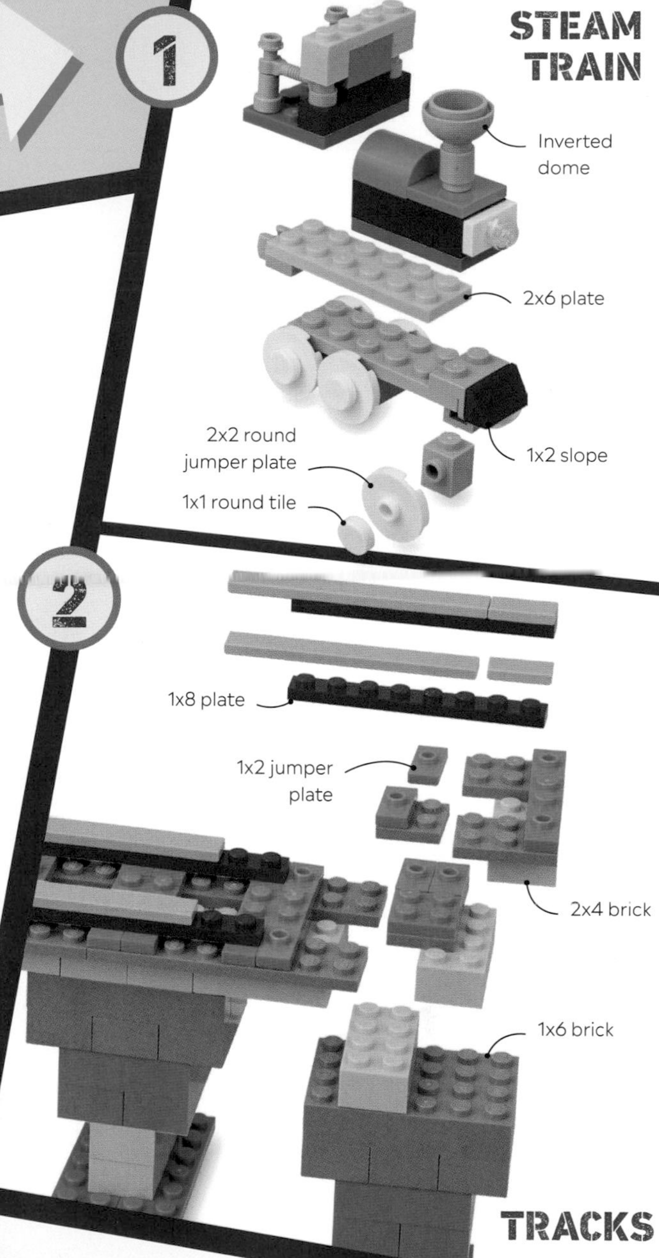
STEAM TRAIN
Inverted dome
2x6 plate
2x2 round jumper plate
1x2 slope
1x1 round tile
2
1x8 plate
1x2 jumper plate
2x4 brick
1x6 brick
TRACKS

STEAM

In old-fashioned steam trains, boiling water creates steam to power the train. The steam pushes parts inside the engine that turn the train wheels to make it move.

Tiles look like smooth rails

2

KEEP GOING!

Charlie gets off the train. He leaps over to the kitchen counter on his skateboard, but the knight jumps across with ease. Run!

QUICK, CHARLIE!

FAREWELL, SIR!

SINK OR SWIM

Charlie dashes across the counter and heads toward the kitchen sink. The knight is right behind him! Suddenly, the adventurer skids to a halt. How will Charlie build his way across this perilous pit in a hurry?

THE PLAN = ?

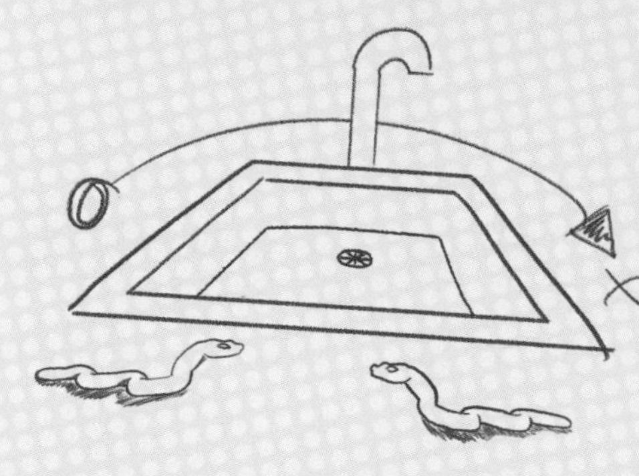

OBSTACLES

SHARP-TOOTHED SNAKES

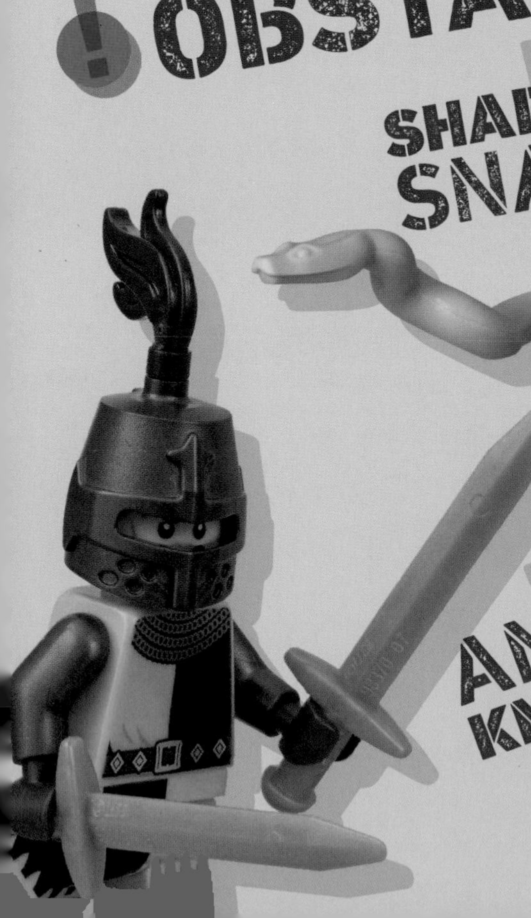

ANGRY KNIGHT

HUNGRY SHARKS

1X4 PLATE

1X1 ROUND BRICK

1X1 ROUND PLATE

2X4 PLATE

2X4 BRICK

YOU'LL HAVE TO GO OVER THE SINK.

USEFUL BRICKS

BRIDGE

DOLPHIN TO RIDE

BUILDING IDEAS

FISHING BOAT

. . . THAT'S IT!

A bridge will get Charlie across the deep hole and keep him away from sharp teeth and sneaky snakes. The knight's heavy armor slows him down, giving Charlie time to quickly cross over the sink.

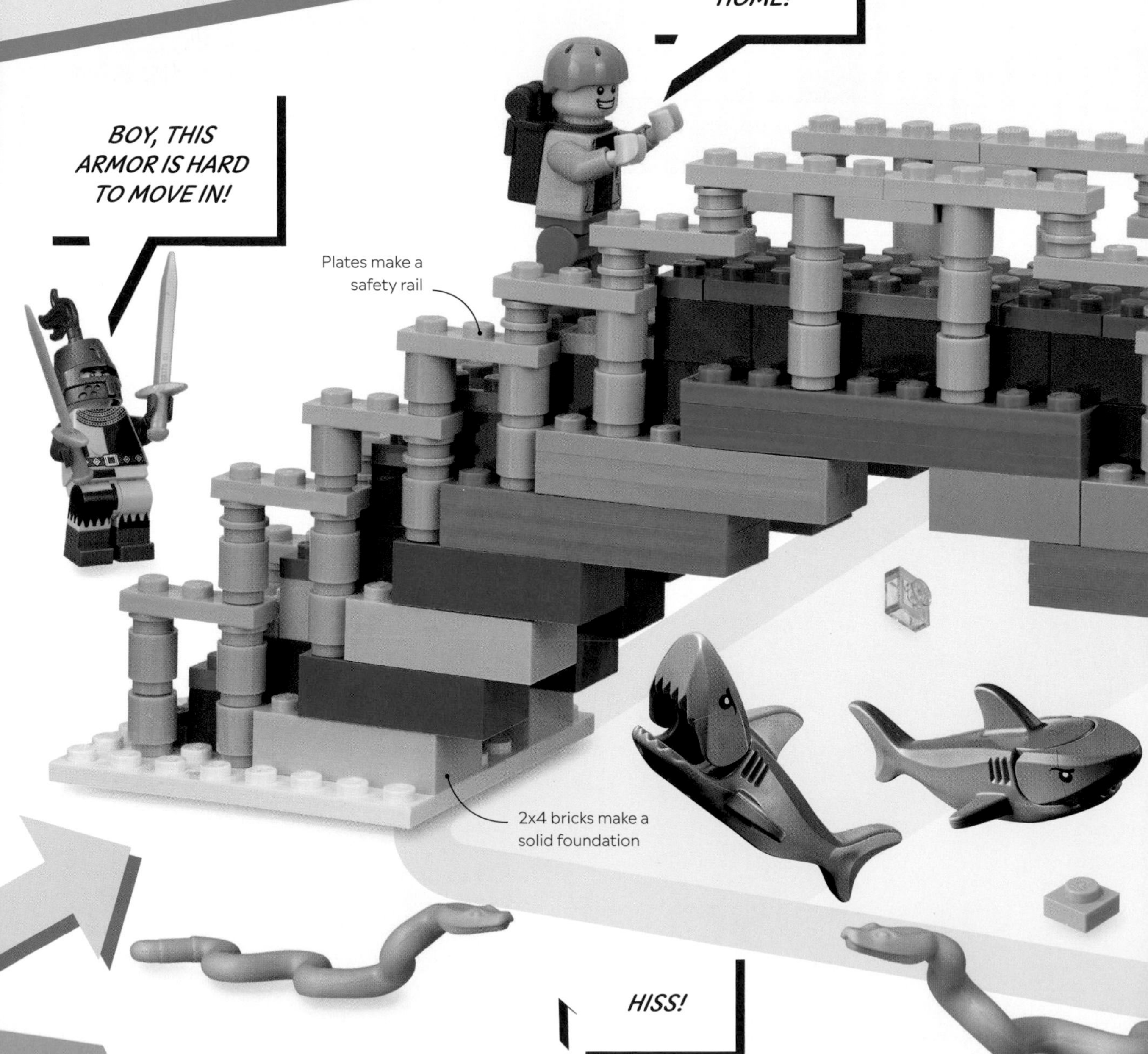

ONE STEP CLOSER TO HOME!
BOY, THIS ARMOR IS HARD TO MOVE IN!
Plates make a safety rail
2x4 bricks make a solid foundation
HISS!

HOW TO BUILD!

1 STEPS

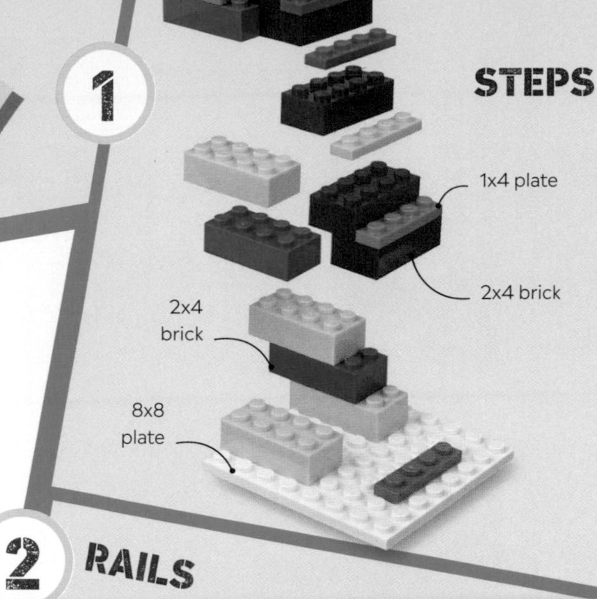
1x4 plate
2x4 brick
2x4 brick
8x8 plate

2 RAILS

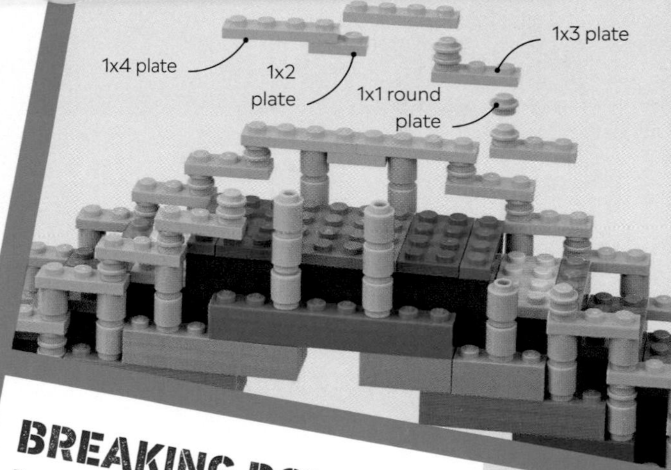
1x4 plate
1x2 plate
1x1 round plate
1x3 plate

ARCHES

Charlie's weight is spread through the bridge's arch. Each side takes the load of the arch and Charlie's weight so the bridge does not collapse.

Create colorful steps with plates

2

1
Stack 1x1 round bricks to form pillars

BREAKING DOWN

Just after Charlie leaps onto the counter, a shark jumps up and knocks the bridge over. The knight is stranded.

THIS MISSION IS FULL OF UPS AND DOWNS!

FLOAT OFF

Charlie is close to the living room now! As he races along the counter, he slips on a wedge of cheese and skids into a tall tower of cookbooks. The book avalanche pushes him to the edge of the counter. The only way is down!

THE PLAN = ?

OBSTACLES

STACK OF BOOKS

STINKY CHEESE

LEGO® TECHNIC HALF PIN

1X1X5 BRICK

BUILDING IDEAS

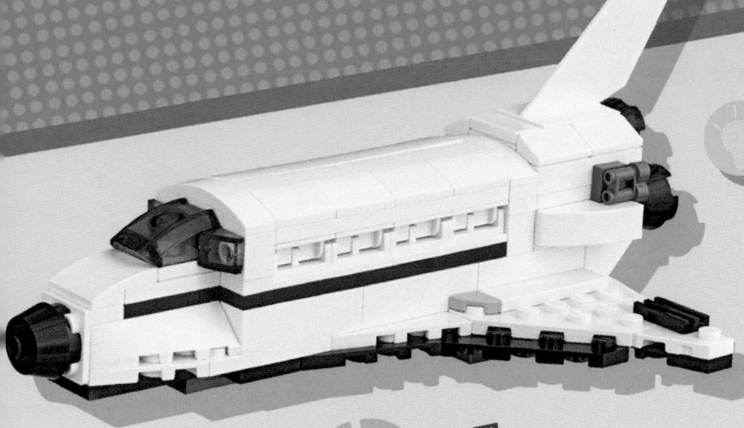

SPACE SHUTTLE

HOT-AIR BALLOON

FLYING UNICORN

IT'S A LONG WAY DOWN, CHARLIE!

USEFUL BRICKS

1X6 ARCH

TELESCOPE

. . . THAT'S IT!

Charlie builds a hot-air balloon and flies toward the doorway. He hopes to float all the way back to the toy shelf where his friends are waiting to greet him. Now to get that cheese off his foot. Yuck!

I'VE BOOKED MY RIDE HOME!

Widest layer of the balloon is in the middle

Rainbow stripes on balloon

Tall bricks link the balloon and basket

Square basket carries minifigure and engine

HOW TO BUILD!

Balloon has a flat top made of thin plates
2
1
Propeller spins using a LEGO Technic connection

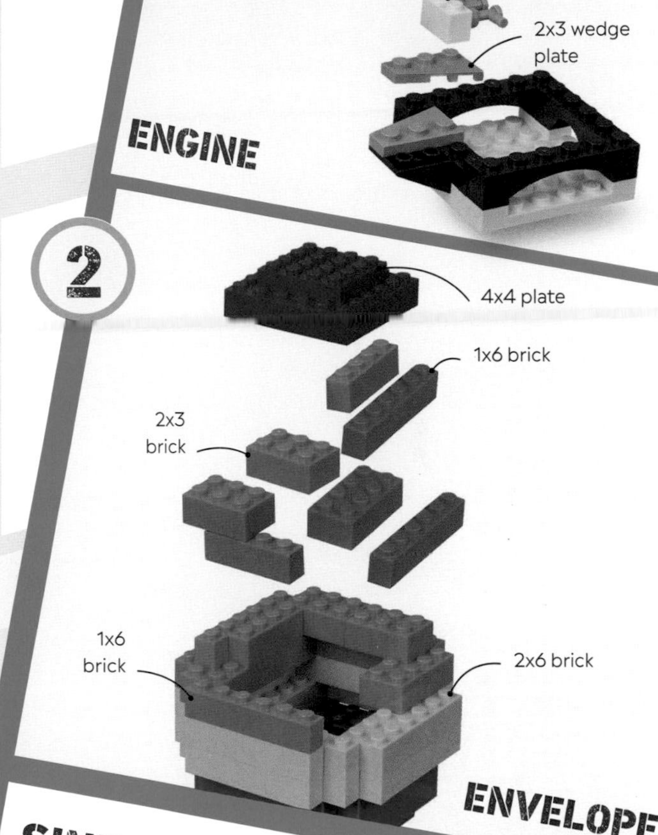

1
LEGO® Technic half pin
1x1 brick with clip
1x2 brick with side studs
2x3 wedge plate
ENGINE
2
4x4 plate
1x6 brick
2x3 brick
1x6 brick
2x6 brick
ENVELOPE

SINKING FEELING

Charlie realizes that he's not as high up as he was when he set off. Is he heading downward?

WHAT A LETDOWN!

HEAT

Warm air inside a hot-air balloon's envelope helps it rise into the air. The pilot slowly lets air out of the balloon to travel downward.

PIECE IT TOGETHER

The hot-air balloon does not stay airborne for long. It slowly floats toward the kitchen floor. Charlie tries to fly upward but it's no use. *Bump*! The balloon lands near something shiny, which gives Charlie a time-traveling idea.

THE PLAN = ?

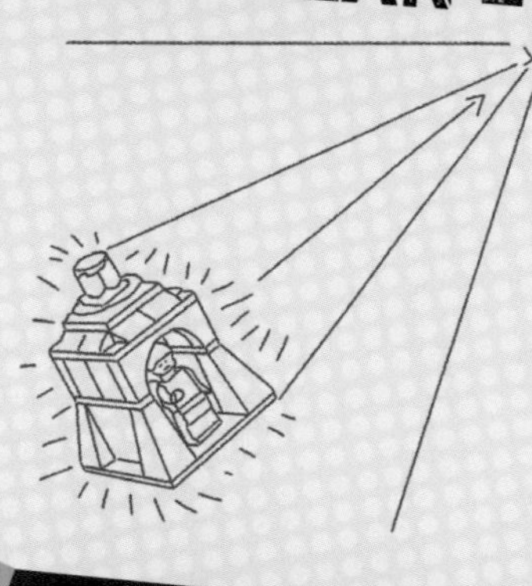

WHAT'S THAT?

TIME

SPACE

AHA! I'VE GOT A BRIGHT IDEA.

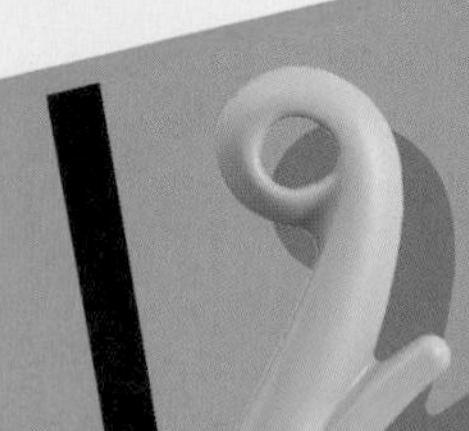

USEFUL BRICKS

1X2 TRANSPARENT BRICK

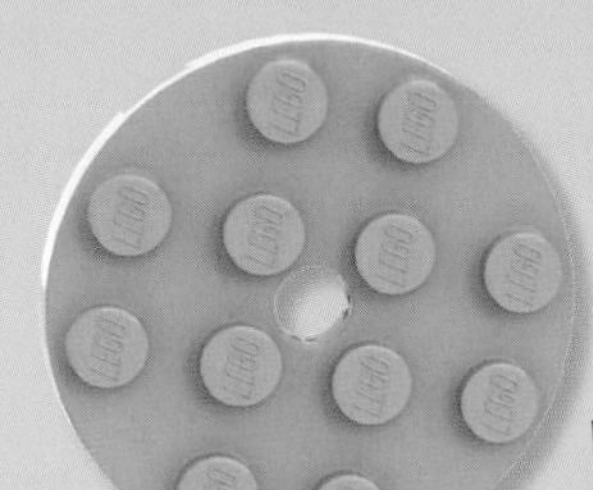

4X4 ROUND PLATE WITH HOLE

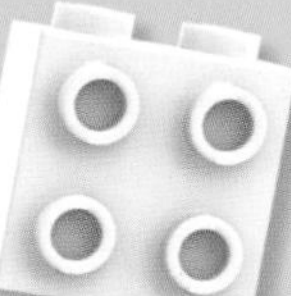

1X2X2 BRICK WITH SIDE STUDS

2X2X3 CORNER SLOPE

I'LL GET BACK IN NO TIME!

TELEPORTER

BUILDING IDEA

. . . THAT'S IT!

Charlie can build a teleporter to get himself back to the bedroom. He sets to work making the cool contraption. Charlie steps inside just as a thieving cyborg approaches. Charlie sets a course for the toy shelf and presses a button . . .

1
I WAS GOING TO USE THAT!
NOT THIS TIME!
Small transparent pieces represent time and space
Transparent bricks for windows
Bricks and slopes form walls

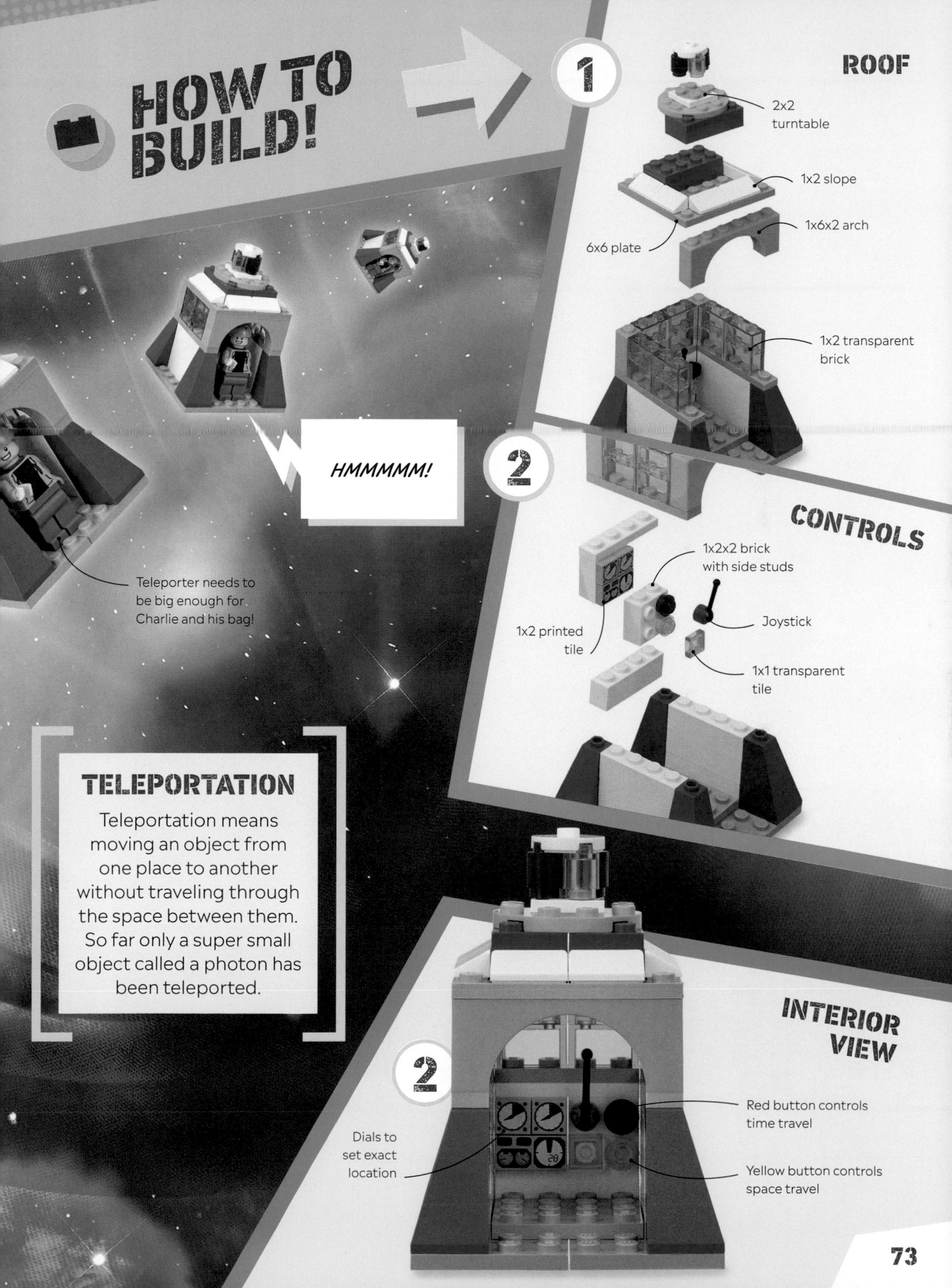
HOW TO BUILD!
1
ROOF
2x2 turntable
1x2 slope
1x6x2 arch
6x6 plate
1x2 transparent brick
HMMMMM!
Teleporter needs to be big enough for Charlie and his bag!
2
CONTROLS
1x2x2 brick with side studs
Joystick
1x2 printed tile
1x1 transparent tile
INTERIOR VIEW
2
Red button controls time travel
Dials to set exact location
Yellow button controls space travel

TELEPORTATION

Teleportation means moving an object from one place to another without traveling through the space between them. So far only a super small object called a photon has been teleported.

CHAPTER 4
LIVING ROOM

HEAD INTO THE LIVING ROOM.
LET'S GO HOME TOGETHER!

THIS ADVENTURE
WILL BE MORE FUN
WITH A FRIEND!
LIVING
ROOM

PURR-FECT GETAWAY

The teleporter bounces into the living room. Oops! Charlie pressed the wrong button. He heads in the direction of the bedroom, but what's that noise? Yikes! There are hungry lions in the way. How can he escape?

THE PLAN = ?

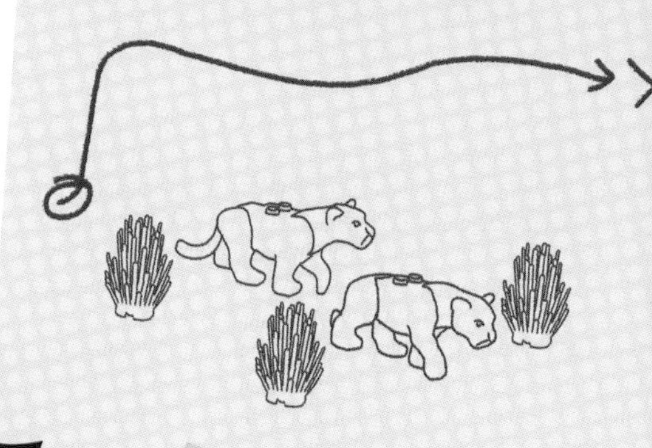

OBSTACLES

HUNGRY LIONS

SPIKY PLANTS

1X10 PLATE

1X2 INVERTED SLOPE

4X4 PLATE

2X2 JUMPER PLATE

1X2 PRINTED TILE

I NEVER WAS VERY GOOD AT QUANTUM PHYSICS . . .

USEFUL BRICKS

DISTRACTING MOUSE

HELICOPTER

NEVER MIND. YOU NEED TO GET AWAY FROM THOSE LIONS!

BUILDING IDEAS

. . . THAT'S IT!

A helicopter will help Charlie escape from the hungry predators and get back to the toy shelf! But as Charlie flies toward the bedroom, the helicopter wobbles. He will have to make an emergency landing . . .

Hold rotor blades in place with a 2x2 round plate
2
Slopes look like a tail fin
Slope
I'M NOT "LION" AROUND HERE!
1
Long plates make landing skids
ROAR!

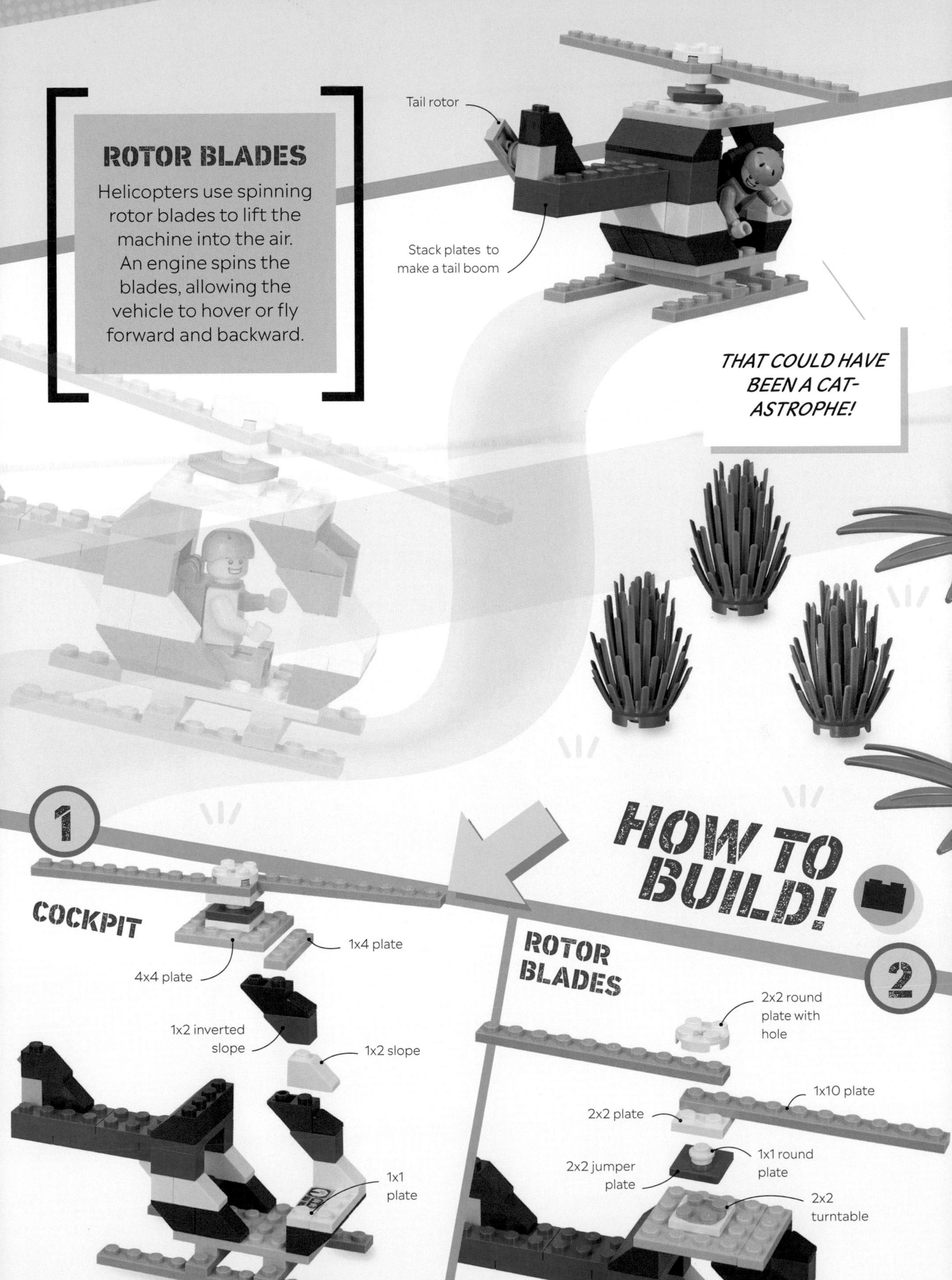
ROTOR BLADES
Helicopters use spinning rotor blades to lift the machine into the air. An engine spins the blades, allowing the vehicle to hover or fly forward and backward.
Tail rotor
Stack plates to make a tail boom
THAT COULD HAVE BEEN A CAT-ASTROPHE!
HOW TO BUILD!
1
COCKPIT
4x4 plate
1x4 plate
1x2 inverted slope
1x2 slope
1x1 plate
2
ROTOR BLADES
2x2 round plate with hole
1x10 plate
2x2 plate
1x1 round plate
2x2 jumper plate
2x2 turntable

HOP TO IT!

Charlie lands by the sofa,
but there is a vacuum cleaner
blocking his way. Charlie will have
to go under the sofa to get past
it. All the dust here is making him
sneeze. How can Charlie move
these big dust bunnies away?

THE PLAN = ?

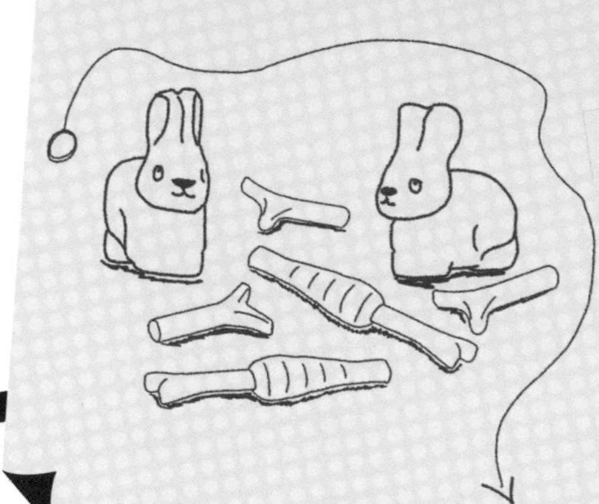

2X4 BRICK

1X2 JUMPER PLATE

1X1 TILE

1X6 BRICK

1X1 PLATE WITH CLIP

SOME BUNNY HAS MADE A LOT OF DUST.

USEFUL
BRICKS

OBSTACLES

DIRTY DUST BUNNIES

SLIPPERY CARROT TOPS

I'VE GOT AN A-MAZE-ING IDEA!

BUILDING IDEAS

DANCING CARROT DISTRACTION

MAZE AND TRAP

. . . THAT'S IT!

Charlie leads the dust bunnies through a maze dotted with carrots and into a trap. Once they eat all the carrots, the bunnies can leave the trap. For now, there is no dust to slow Charlie down. He hurries off.

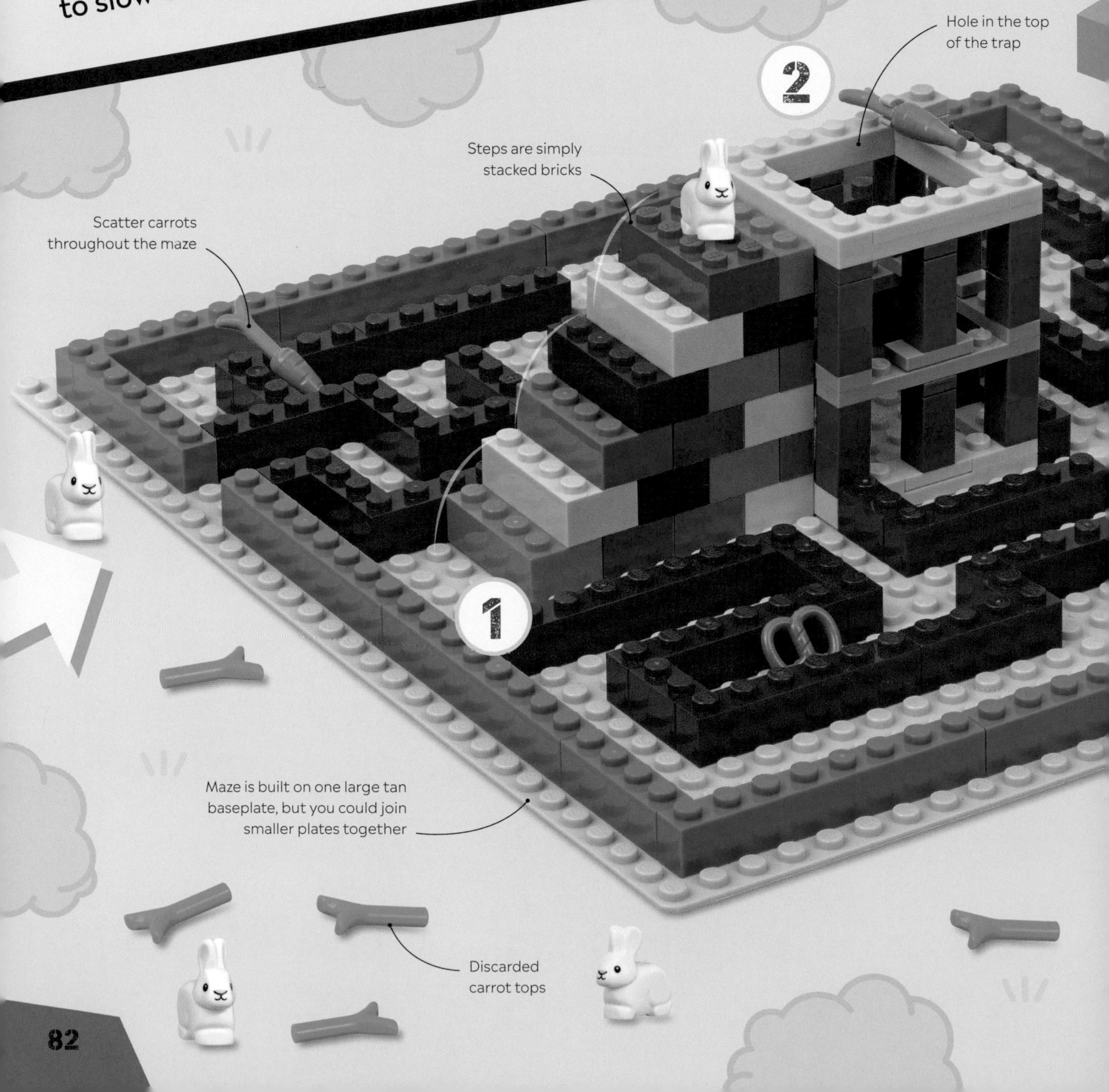

Hole in the top of the trap

2

Steps are simply stacked bricks

Scatter carrots throughout the maze

1

Maze is built on one large tan baseplate, but you could join smaller plates together

Discarded carrot tops

OPTICAL ILLUSIONS

An optical illusion is something that tricks your eyes. The bunnies thought they were bouncing straight onto a carrot, not into a trap!

WHAT'S THAT?

It's dark under the sofa, and Charlie bumps into something. Is it a monster?

Use any food pieces that might have fallen under the sofa!

Long, thin bricks form maze border

THAT WAS HARE RAISING!

HOW TO BUILD!

1 STEPS

1x4 brick

2x4 brick

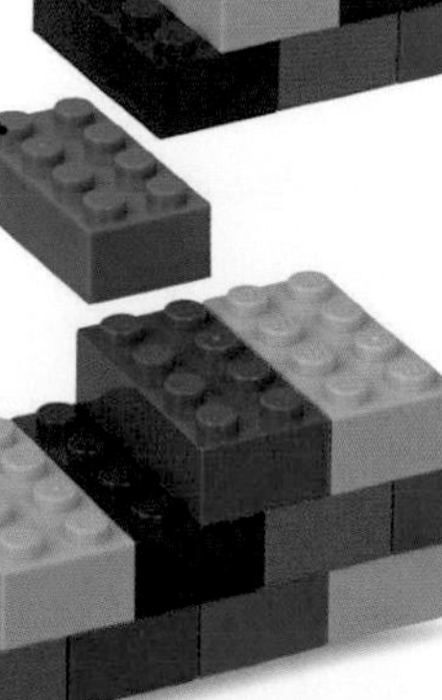

2 TRAP

1x6 plate

1x4 plate

1x1 tile

1x2 jumper plate

1x1 brick

MOVING UP

Phew! It's not a monster. It's Charlie's friend Maya, who has been lost under the sofa. Now the pair can work together to get back to the toy shelf. First, they need to get up to the sofa to make it past the vacuum cleaner.

THE PLAN = ?

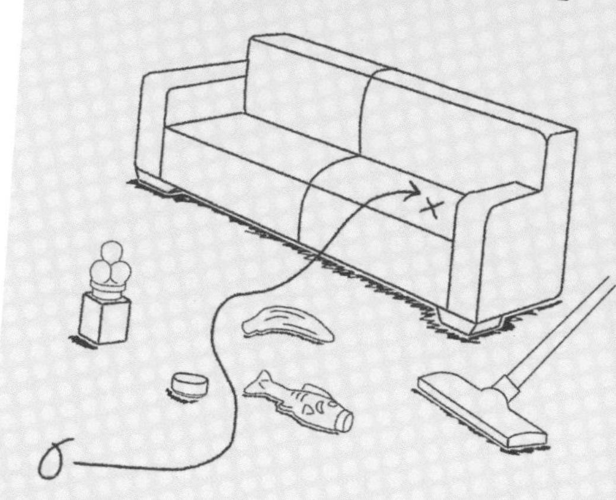

OBSTACLES

STINKY TRASH

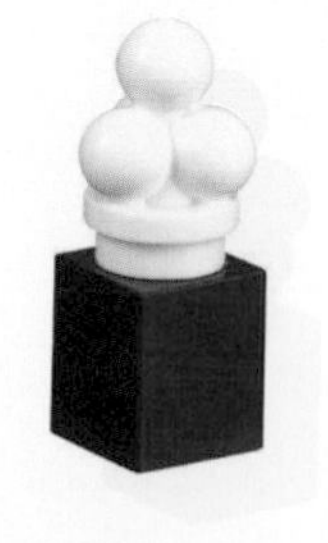

LET'S HELP EACH OTHER GET HOME.

GREAT IDEA!

LEGO® TECHNIC
FOUR BLADE ROTOR

2X2 BRICK
WITH PIN

2X2 SLOPE

2X10 PLATE

TWO HEADS ARE BETTER THAN ONE!

USEFUL BRICKS

WINDMILL TO RIDE

TREE TO CLIMB

STACK OF SUSHI TO SCALE

BUILDING IDEAS

...THAT'S IT!

Maya and Charlie build a windmill, but the vacuum cleaner is getting closer! They each grab a windmill blade and ride it to the sofa. They bounce across to the other side of the sofa and out of harm's way.

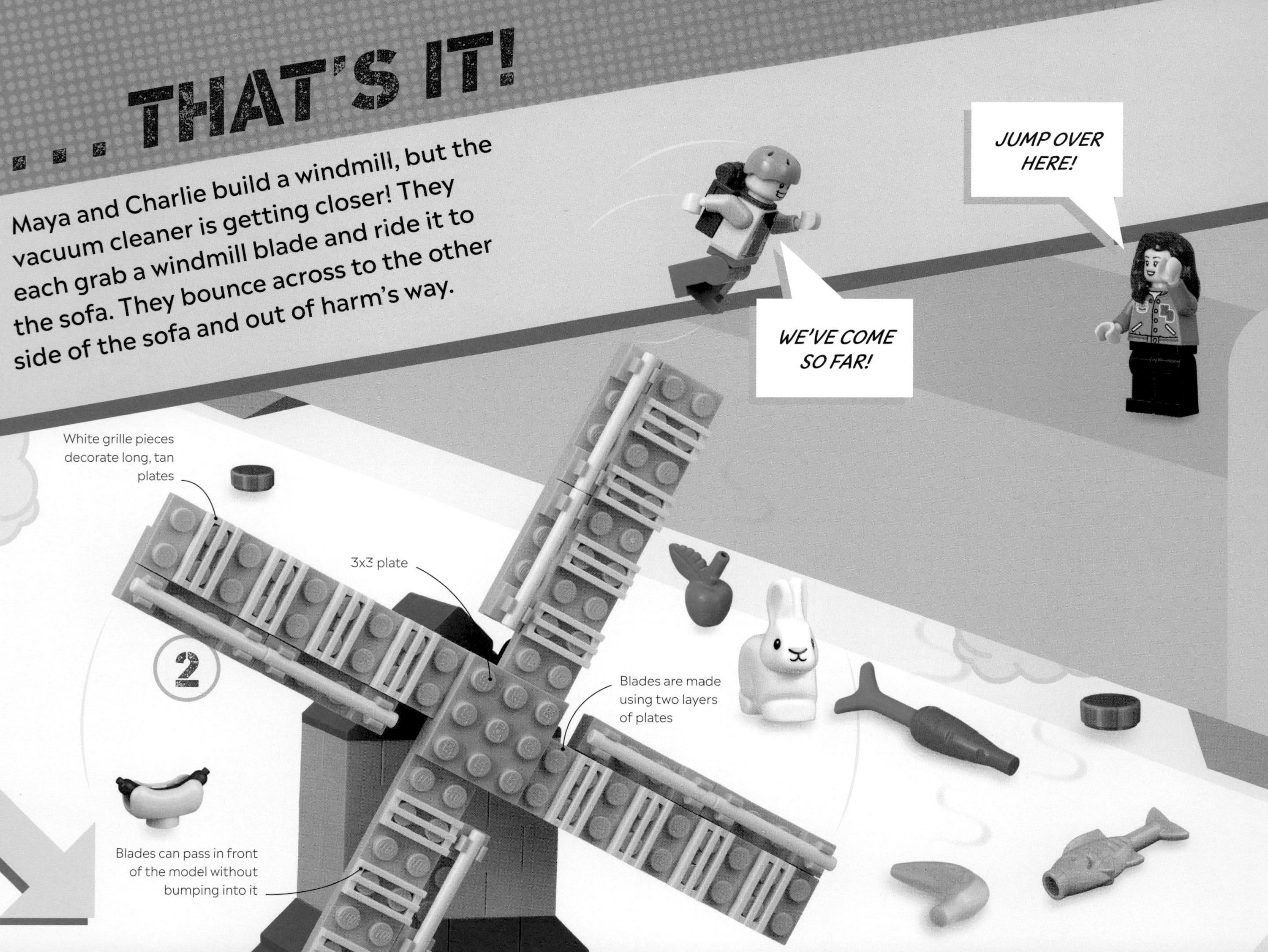

WE'VE COME SO FAR!
JUMP OVER HERE!
2
White grille pieces decorate long, tan plates
3x3 plate
Blades are made using two layers of plates
Blades can pass in front of the model without bumping into it

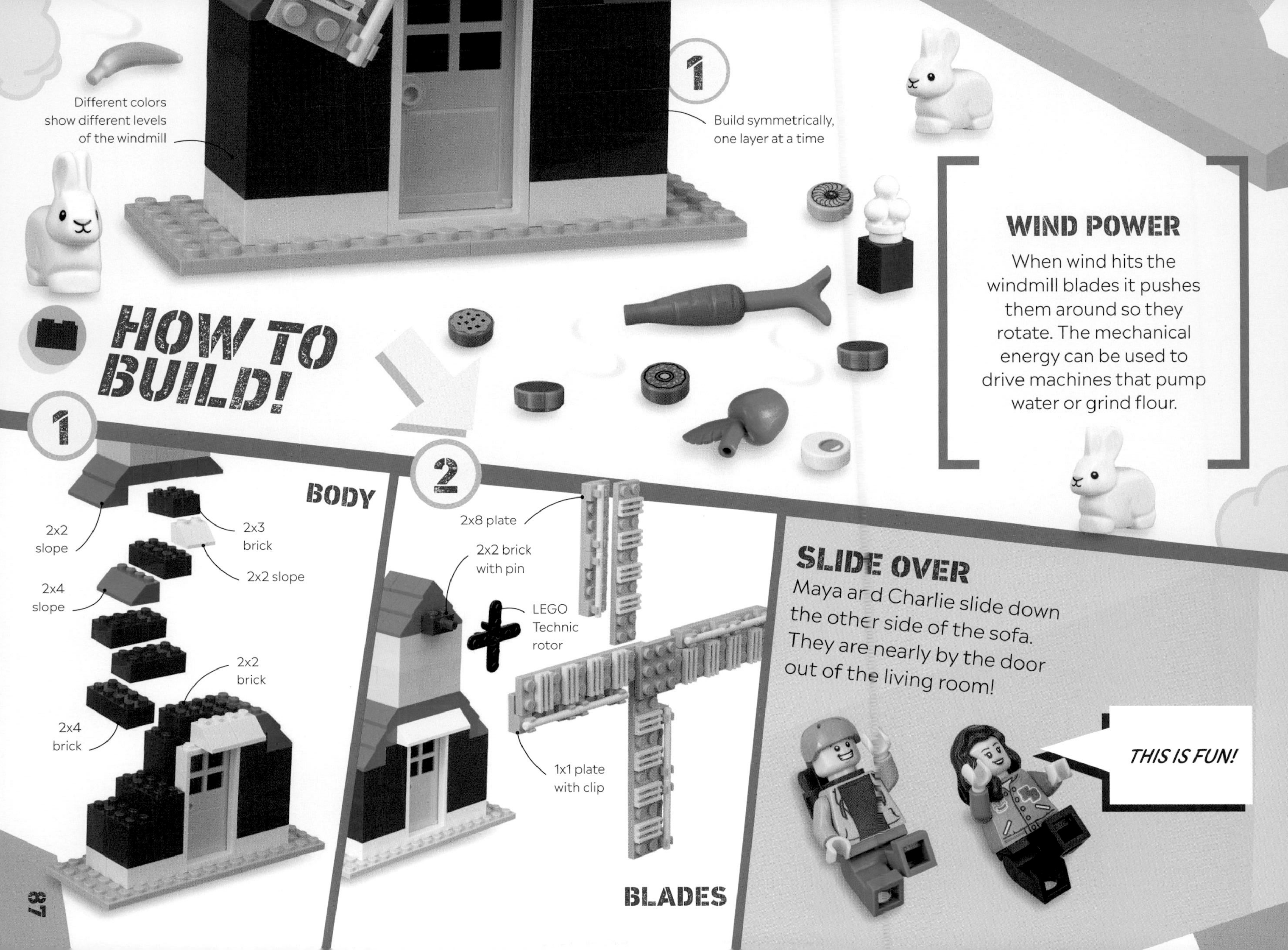
Different colors show different levels of the windmill
Build symmetrically, one layer at a time
1
HOW TO BUILD!
1
BODY
2x2 slope
2x3 brick
2x2 slope
2x4 slope
2x2 brick
2x4 brick
2
BLADES
2x8 plate
2x2 brick with pin
LEGO Technic rotor
1x1 plate with clip
THIS IS FUN!

WIND POWER

When wind hits the windmill blades it pushes them around so they rotate. The mechanical energy can be used to drive machines that pump water or grind flour.

SLIDE OVER

Maya and Charlie slide down the other side of the sofa. They are nearly by the door out of the living room!

ON THE MOVE

Suddenly, music blares. A group of noisy party animals surrounds Charlie and Maya. The persistent party-goers want the adventurers to join in with their singing and dancing. Maya and Charlie want to go home. What will they do?

THE PLAN = ?

OBSTACLES

PARTY ANIMALS

2X2 BRICK

2X12 PLATE

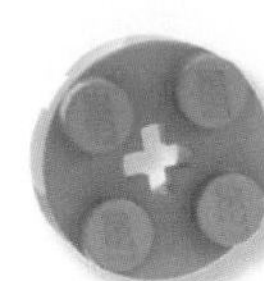

2X2 ROUND PLATE WITH HOLE

2X6 DOUBLE INVERTED SLOPE

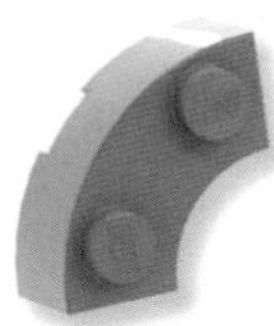

2X2 ROUND CORNER BRICK

USEFUL BRICKS

IT'S TIME TO LEAVE THIS PARTY!

OBSTACLE COURSE

DRAGON TO SCARE THEM

BUILDING IDEAS

. . . THAT'S IT!

Maya and Charlie construct an obstacle course to slow down the party animals while the pair jump, crawl, and climb away. The party animals can't fit their bulky costumes through the tunnel at the end.

HOW TO BUILD!

MOMENTUM

Momentum keeps the merry-go-round spinning for a short time even after Charlie and Maya stop pushing it. All moving objects have momentum.

1

Slope looks like a seat

Plate spins on a 2x2 turntable

Attach the merry-go-round to a baseplate

I'M NOT "DRAGON" MYSELF ON THAT!

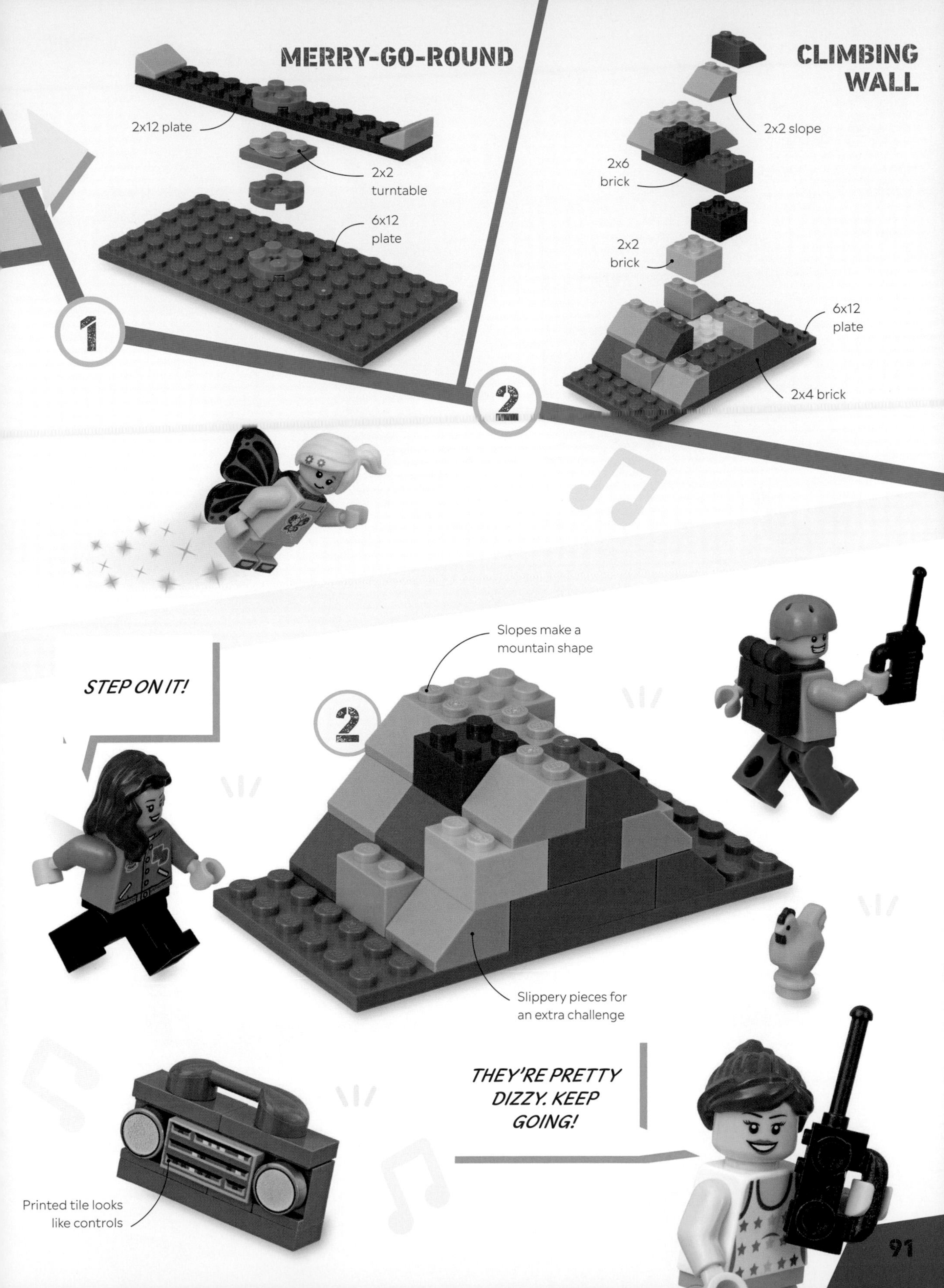

MERRY-GO-ROUND
2x12 plate
2x2 turntable
6x12 plate
1
CLIMBING WALL
2x2 slope
2x6 brick
2x2 brick
6x12 plate
2x4 brick
2
Slopes make a mountain shape
STEP ON IT!
2
Slippery pieces for an extra challenge
THEY'RE PRETTY DIZZY. KEEP GOING!
Printed tile looks like controls

KEEP GOING!

THIS IS A "HOLE" NEW CHALLENGE.

I DON'T THINK THEY CAN FIT THROUGH THE TUNNEL!

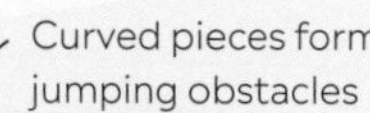

Curved pieces form jumping obstacles

Fill the rings with slippery tiles

1

HOW TO BUILD!

1

RING HOP

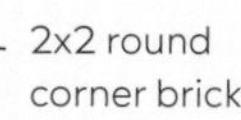

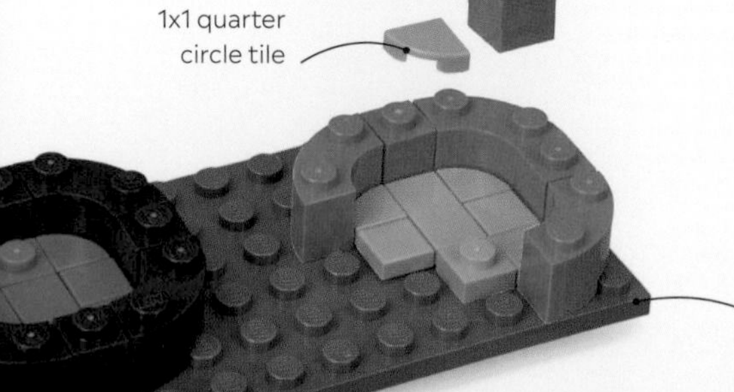

1x1 brick
2x2 round corner brick
1x1 quarter circle tile
6x12 plate

2

TUNNEL

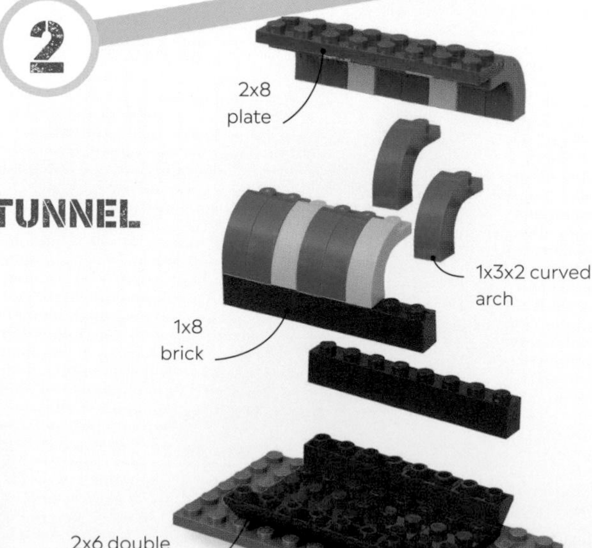

2x8 plate
1x3x2 curved arch
1x8 brick
2x6 double inverted slope

MEASURING

Charlie and Maya build the tunnel so it is too narrow for the party animals to fit through. Measurements can help you decide how big or small something, like a LEGO® model, should be.

ROCK ON

Phew! The party is over but the mission isn't. Maya and Charlie carry on. But what's that smell?

HURRY UP!

I'M STUCK!

2

Plate forms the roof of the tunnel

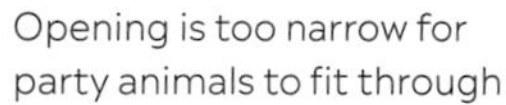
Opening is too narrow for party animals to fit through

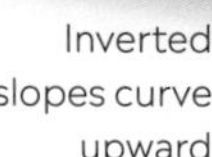
Inverted slopes curve upward

THAT WAS A WILD PARTY.

LET'S GET OUT OF HERE!

BLAST OFF!

Charlie and Maya reach the other side of the living room. The bedroom is just across the hall, but it's a real pigsty over here! How will they get around it? Then, Maya spots an abandoned rocket that might just work . . .

THE PLAN = ?

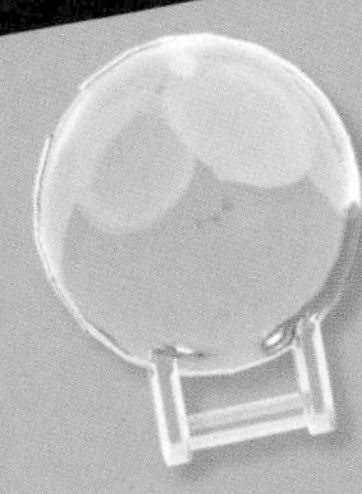

TRANSPARENT DOME WINDSCREEN

3X3X2 CONE

1X1 PLATE WITH CLIP

1X6X2 ARCH

USEFUL BRICKS

LET'S REBUILD THIS SHIP!

WE CAN ROCK IT!

OBSTACLES

PIGS

ROTTING FRUIT

OOZY MUD

ROCKET SHIP

USE YOUR REBUILDING SKILLS!

BUILDING IDEA

. . . THAT'S IT!

Maya and Charlie mend the abandoned rocket. The adventurers blast off over the pigsty toward the bedroom. Maya and Charlie are so close to home now. They can't wait to be reunited with their friends!

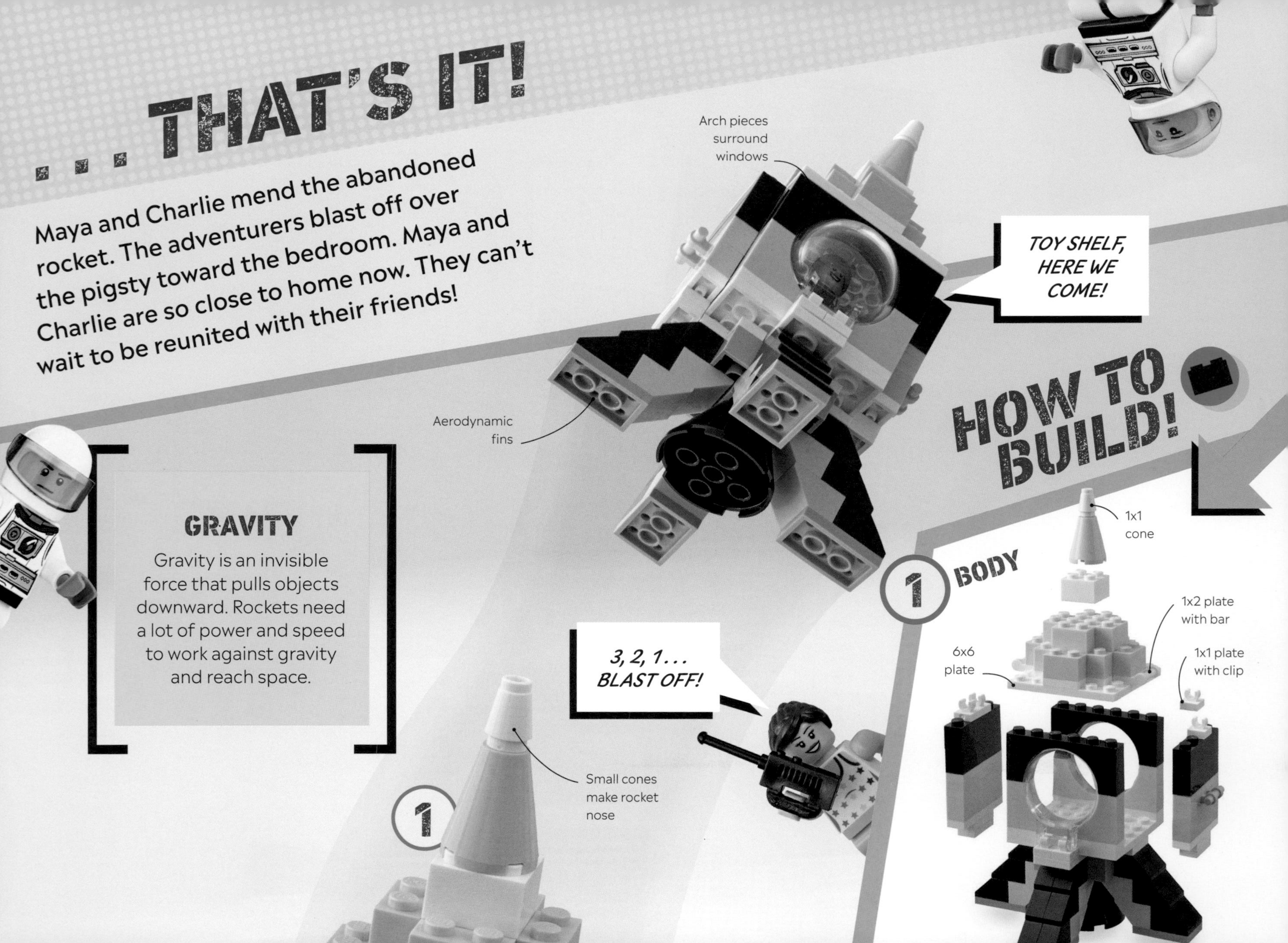

Arch pieces surround windows
TOY SHELF, HERE WE COME!
Aerodynamic fins
HOW TO BUILD!
1 BODY
1x1 cone
1x2 plate with bar
6x6 plate
1x1 plate with clip
3, 2, 1... BLAST OFF!
Small cones make rocket nose
1

GRAVITY

Gravity is an invisible force that pulls objects downward. Rockets need a lot of power and speed to work against gravity and reach space.

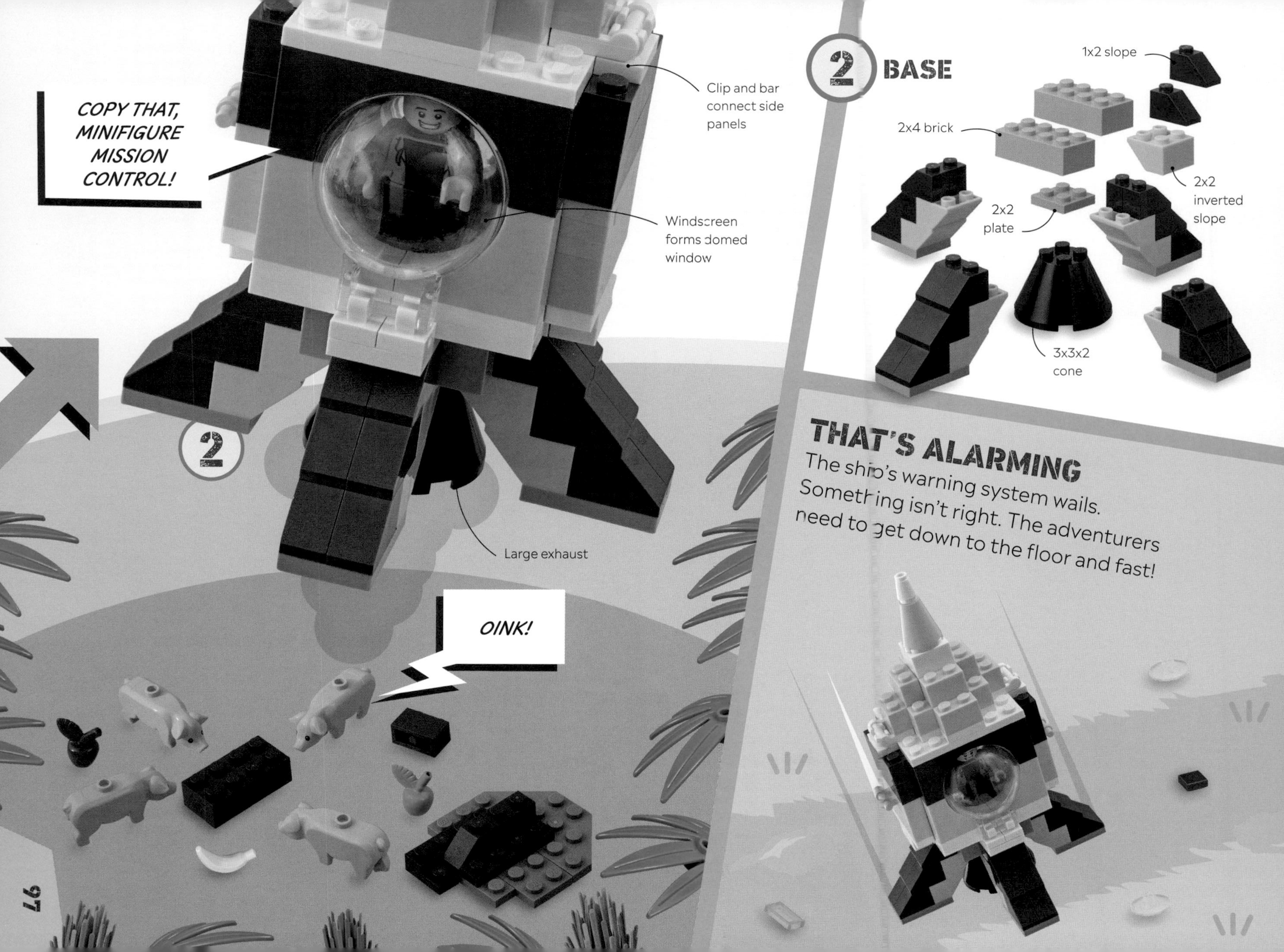
COPY THAT, MINIFIGURE MISSION CONTROL!
Clip and bar connect side panels
Windscreen forms domed window
2
Large exhaust
OINK!
2 BASE
1x2 slope
2x4 brick
2x2 inverted slope
2x2 plate
3x3x2 cone

THAT'S ALARMING

The ship's warning system wails. Something isn't right. The adventurers need to get down to the floor and fast!

CHAPTER 5
BEDROOM

YOU'RE IN THE HOMESTRETCH!
YOU CAN'T OUTFOX ME.
WAIT UP!
BEDROOM

THIS IS A "FAIRY" COOL ADVENTURE!
I CAN SEE THE TOY SHELF FROM HERE!

NO MESSING AROUND

The rocket whooshes into the bedroom and crashes on a soft blanket. At least they are nearly home! Charlie and Maya decide to split up and race back to the shelf. Who will get across the messy floor and back home first?

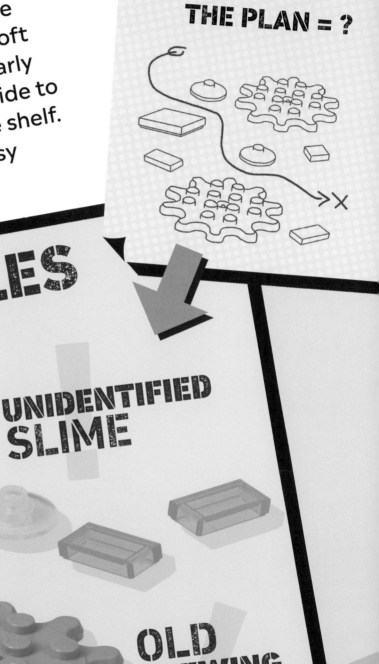

THE PLAN = ?

OBSTACLES

UNIDENTIFIED SLIME

MELTED CHOCOLATE

OLD CHEWING GUM

1X1 BRICK WITH BAR

1X2 PLATE WITH BALL JOINT

1X2 PLATE WITH SOCKET

WHO WILL WIN THE RACE?

1X2 BRICK

1X2 BRICK WITH SIDE STUDS

USEFUL BRICKS

FLIPPERS

BALLOONS TO FLOAT ON

MECH SUIT

BUILDING IDEAS

. . . THAT'S IT!

A strong mech suit is perfect for stepping over the oozy slime, sticky chewing gum, and messy melted chocolate on the floor! Charlie uses the joysticks to steer the mechanical suit toward the toy shelf.

I'LL DEFINITELY GET BACK TO THE SHELF FIRST.

1x2 grille looks like a vent

1

Plates and tiles make strong feet for stepping through all sorts of mess

HOW TO BUILD!

1

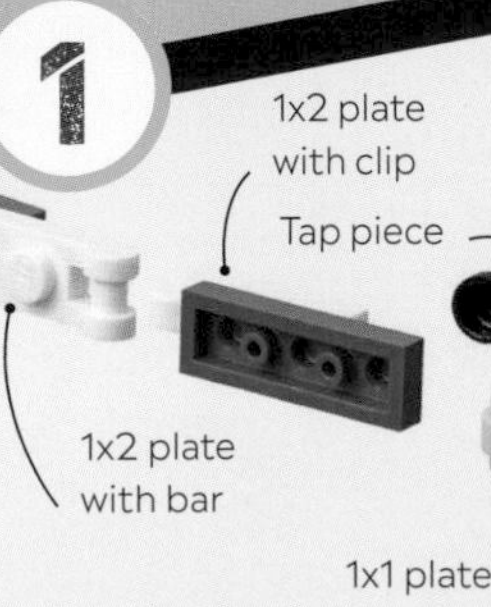

1x2 plate with clip

Tap piece

1x2 plate with bar

1x1 headlight brick

1x1 plate with ring

ARM

2

LEG

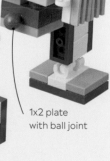

1x2 plate with socket

1x2 plate

1x2 plate with ball joint

1x1 brick with bar

2x2 corner plate

1x1 plate with clip

DON'T FLIP OUT IF I WIN!
PILE OF PROBLEMS
The mech suit is great for crossing the mess but it can't take Charlie over this mound of laundry!
Plates with a bar and clip allow the arms to bend
THIS REALLY SUITS ME.
1x1 plate with clip is a robotic hand
2
MECHANICAL EXOSUITS
These special suits have mechanical parts that act like human muscles. Some exosuits can walk and pick up objects.

THIS STINKS!

The mech suit stops at the foot of a mound of stinky laundry. A huge bear blocks Charlie's way around it. The only way to the toy shelf is to go under the smelly pile. What's the best way to get through the dark, icky place?

THE PLAN = ?

OBSTACLES

POISONOUS MUSHROOMS

GIANT BEAR

HOLD YOUR NOSE!

SMELLY CLOTHES

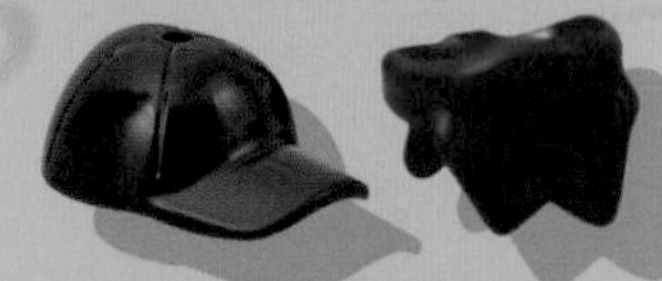

BUILDING IDEAS

MAGICAL DOOR

MINING CART

TUNNEL

USEFUL BRICKS

1X2X5 TRANSPARENT BRICK

1X1 BRICK WITH SIDE STUD

2X2 RADAR DISH

2X2 INVERTED SLOPE

1X2 SLOPE

. . . THAT'S IT!

Charlie builds a tunnel to get through the laundry. Bats, spiders, and scorpions like the long, dark tunnel, but at least the bear can't fit inside! Charlie flicks on his flashlight and strides on. He wonders where Maya is.

I'LL WIN THIS RACE!
Pickax for climbing

GRR!

Plates for the roof
Stacks of bricks form the entrance and exit

HOW TO BUILD!

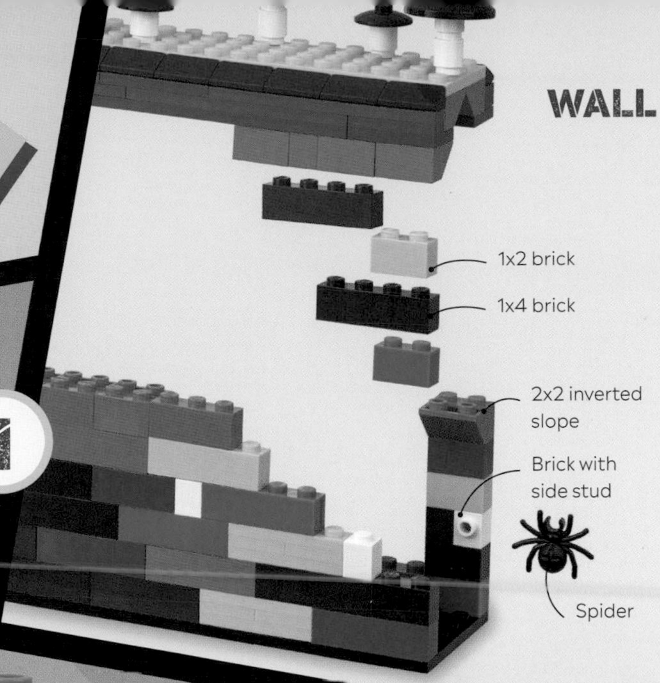

WALL

1x2 brick

1x4 brick

2x2 inverted slope

Brick with side stud

Spider

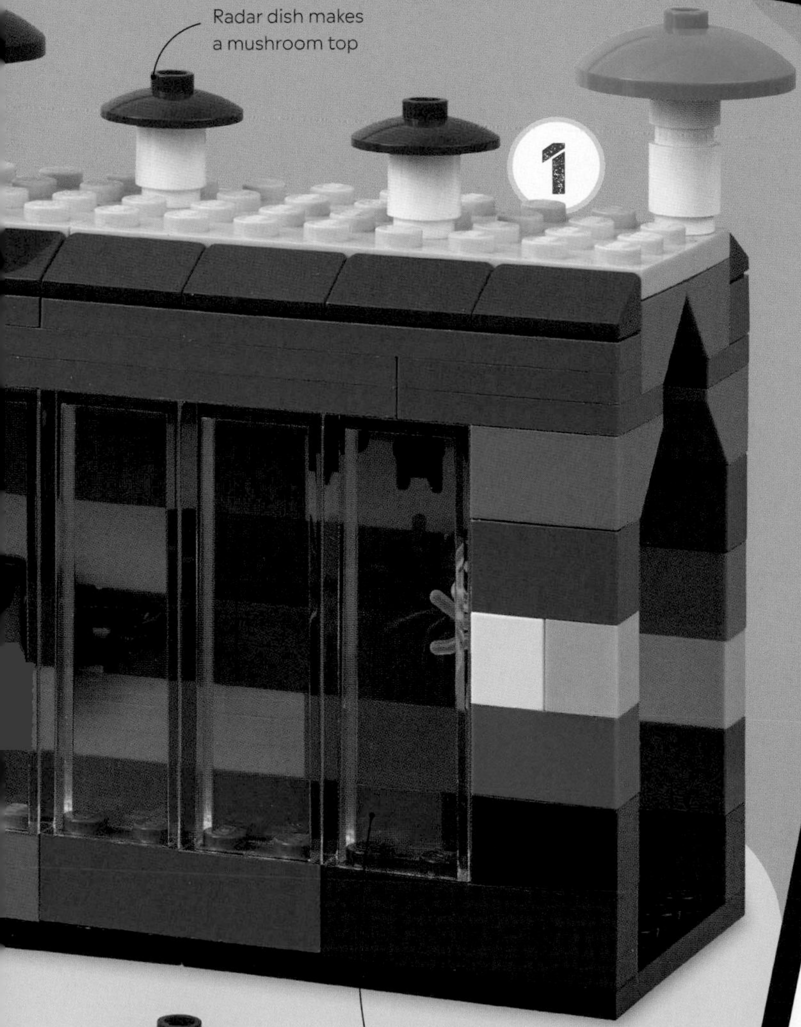

1

Radar dish makes a mushroom top

1

Use transparent pieces so you can see inside the tunnel

MATERIALS

Tunnels are large tubes that are built underground. Tunnels must be built of strong materials inside and out to stop them collapsing.

OUT OF THE DARK

Charlie has made it through the tunnel. He is so close to home, but he senses danger ahead.

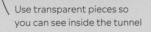

FULL SPEED AHEAD

Charlie emerges from the tunnel by the bed. As he walks past, Charlie spots a warrior, then another, and another! The warriors stop monsters from getting under the bed, and they do not like strangers wandering nearby . . .

THE PLAN = ?

OBSTACLES

DEFENSIVE WARRIORS

I'M NOT HANGING AROUND HERE!

USEFUL BRICKS

WHEEL AND TIRE

2X2 WEDGE PLATE

1X2 GRILLE

2X2 PLATE WITH PINS

1X1 TRANSPARENT SLOPE

BUILDING IDEAS

SKATEBOARD

IT LOOKS LIKE MAYA IS WINNING THE RACE!

RACE CAR

HIGH-SPEED TRAIN

. . . THAT'S IT!

Charlie makes a speedy car and jumps in. He swerves around the Under-the-Bed Warriors. Then he speeds onto a ramp and over their heads. The warriors chase Charlie, but no toy can keep up with this fast race car!

LEAP OVER THE WARRIORS!

1

I'M GETTING A LITTLE JUMPY.

2

Wedge plates for a bumper

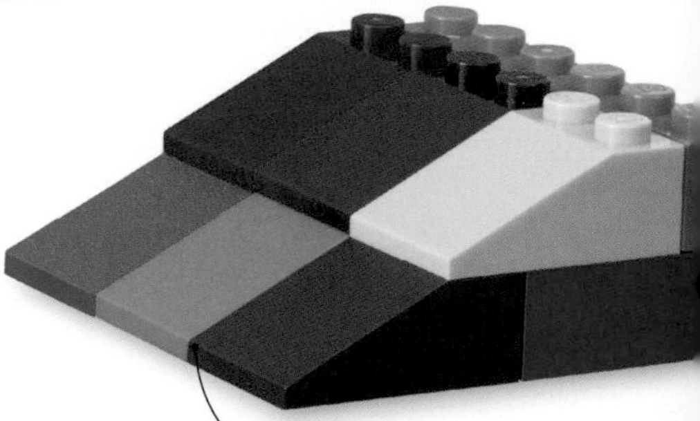

Slopes create a ramp

HOW TO BUILD!

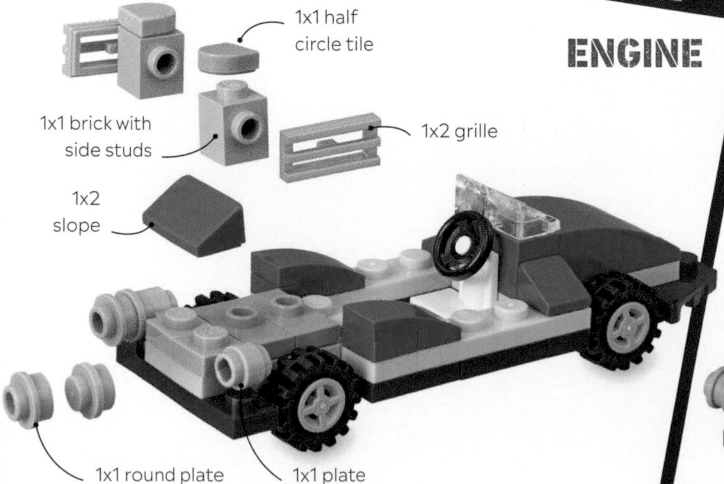

1

ENGINE

1x1 half circle tile

1x1 brick with side studs

1x2 grille

1x2 slope

1x1 round plate with hole

1x1 plate with ring

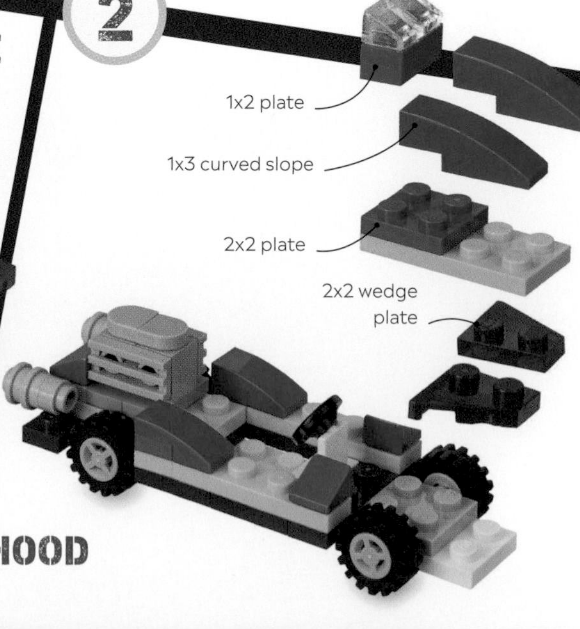

2

1x2 plate

1x3 curved slope

2x2 plate

2x2 wedge plate

HOOD

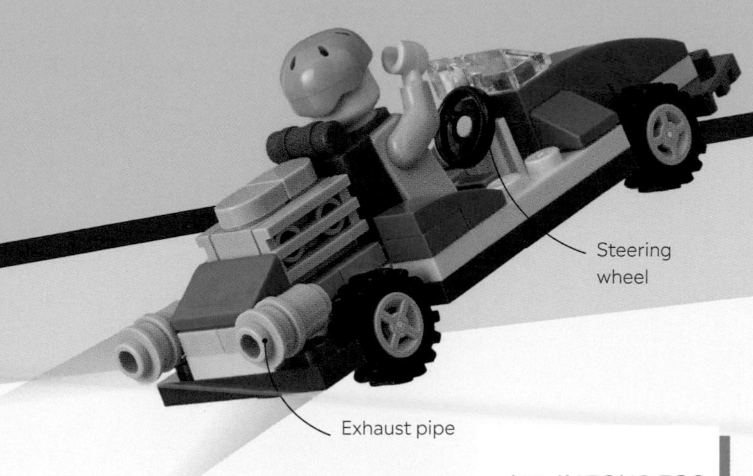
Steering wheel
Exhaust pipe

NO INTRUDERS ALLOWED!
GET OUT OF HERE!
Warriors can't reach Charlie, even with their long weapons!

LAUNCH SPEED

Getting the speed just right is key to making the car "jump" off the ramp. The car can soar through the air only if Charlie's launch speed isn't too slow or too fast.

NEARLY HOME!

Charlie has sped away from the warriors, but he won't be able to drive all the way up to the shelf.

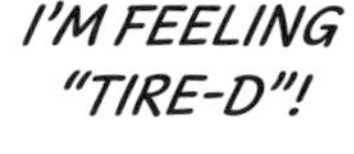

I'M FEELING "TIRE-D"!

STEP UP

Charlie stops the race car and looks up. The toy shelf is just above him. He looks behind him. Oh no! Everyone that has chased him during his mission is right on his tail. How can Charlie get up to the toy shelf as quickly as possible?

THE PLAN = ?

! OBSTACLES

VILLAINS FROM THE MISSION

1X10 BRICK

2X4 BRICK

1X1 BRICK

2X2 BRICK

2X2 PLATE

USEFUL BRICKS

SPIRAL STAIRCASE

YOU'RE ALMOST HOME. DON'T GIVE UP!

CLOUD TO FLOAT ON

BUILDING IDEAS

. . . THAT'S IT!

Charlie makes a spiral staircase and races upward. As he gets near the top, he can hear music getting louder. He must be close to home, but Charlie can't shake the crowd that's following him!

HARD WORK

Climbing the stairs is hard work! In science the word "work" has a special meaning—it means the energy used when a force moves an object.

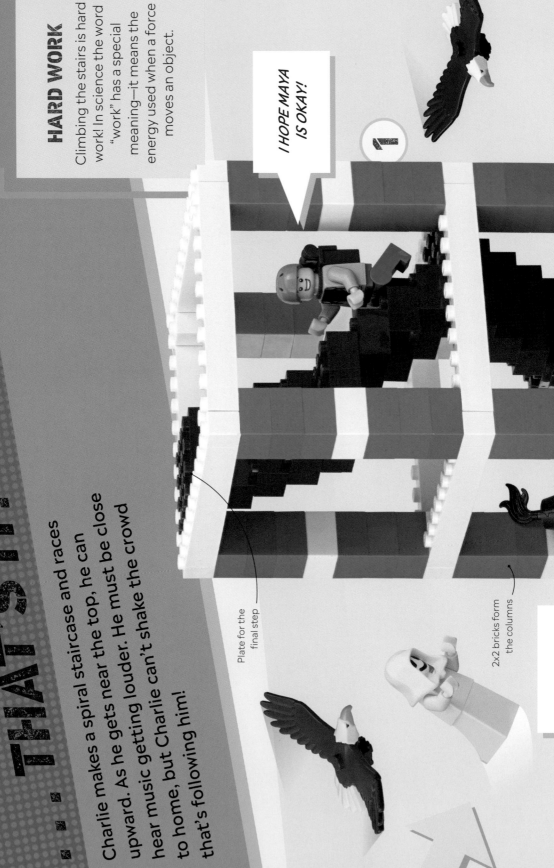

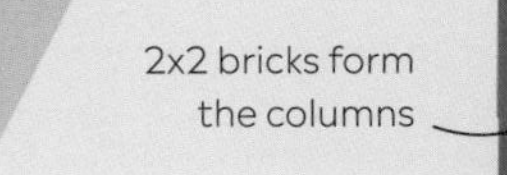

I HOPE MAYA IS OKAY!
NOT SO FAST!
Plate for the final step
2x2 bricks form the columns
1
2

HOW TO BUILD!

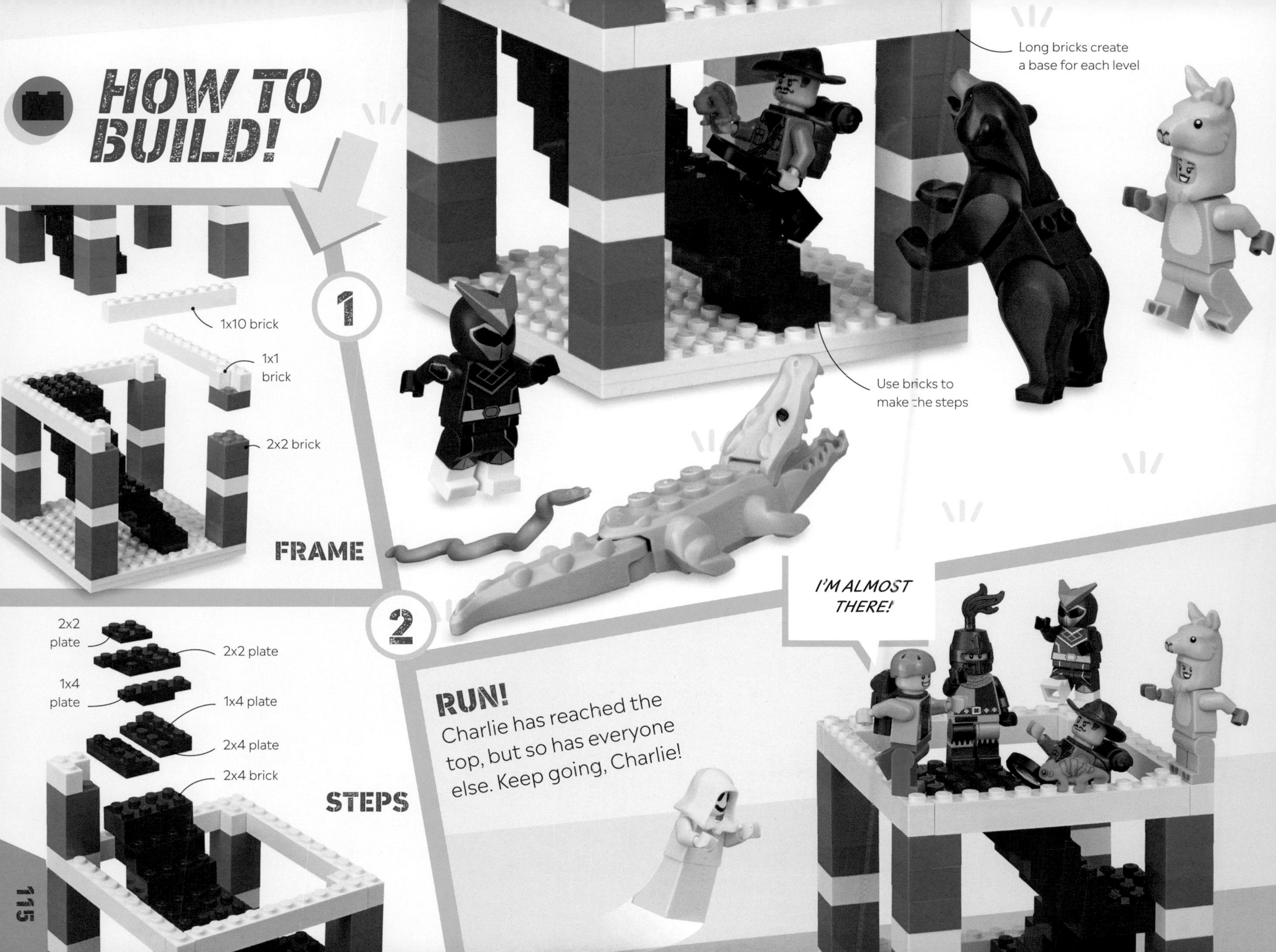
1
FRAME
1x10 brick
1x1 brick
2x2 brick
Long bricks create a base for each level
Use bricks to make the steps
2
STEPS
2x2 plate
2x2 plate
1x4 plate
1x4 plate
2x4 plate
2x4 brick
I'M ALMOST THERE!

RUN!
Charlie has reached the top, but so has everyone else. Keep going, Charlie!

IT'S PARTY TIME!

Hooray! Charlie is back on the toy shelf and so is Maya! Their friends celebrate their return with a party. Charlie is worried about the crowd of toys that has followed him, but they just want to join in the fun. Now it's time to eat pizza, dance, and set off the confetti cannon!

HOW TO BUILD!

DISCO LIGHT

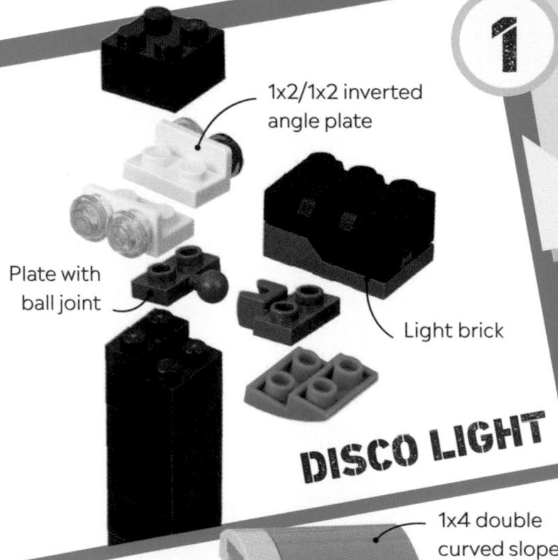

1x2/1x2 inverted angle plate

Plate with ball joint

Light brick

CONFETTI CANNON

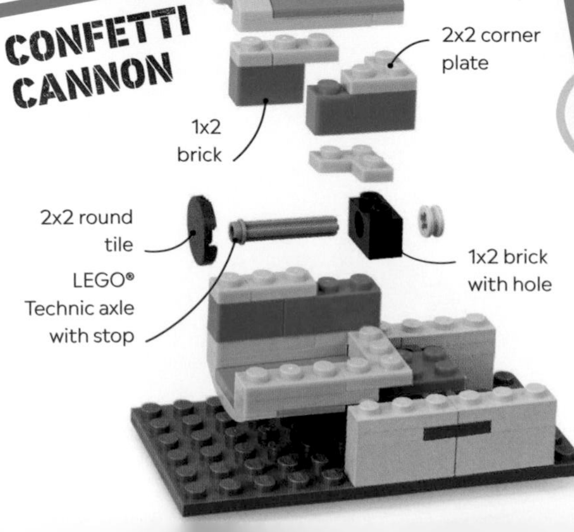

1x4 double curved slope

2x2 corner plate

1x2 brick

2x2 round tile

LEGO® Technic axle with stop

1x2 brick with hole

1

WHO LIKES TO DO THE FOXTROT?

Stack of bricks forms the light stand

Radar dish looks like a speaker

2

WELCOME BACK!

Transparent plates for squares on a dance floor

USEFUL BRICKS

1X2 PLATE WITH SOCKET

1X2 PLATE WITH BALL JOINT

1X2 PLATE WITH SIDE RAIL

1X3 BRICK

1X4 BRICK WITH GROOVE

LIGHT BRICK

BUILDING IDEAS

DJ BOOTH

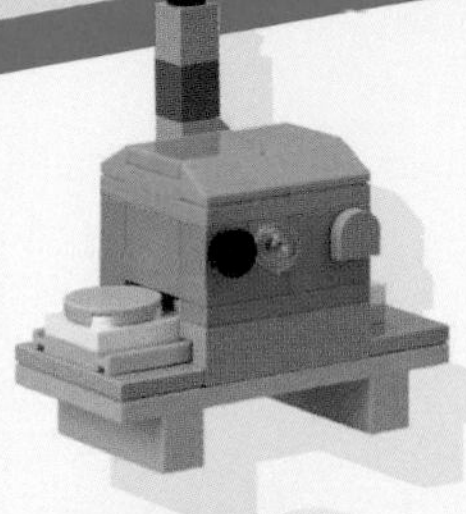

PIZZA OVEN

CONFETTI CANNON

DISCO LIGHTS

DANCE FLOOR

Ball-and-socket joint lets the light move up and down

1x1 round plate for a chimney top

Pizza tray made from a plate

Brick with groove

Plate with rail lets the tray slide out

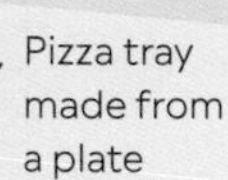

WHAT TOOK YOU SO LONG?

Make confetti with 1x1 round plates

1x6 plate

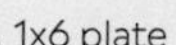

GREAT P-ARR-TY!

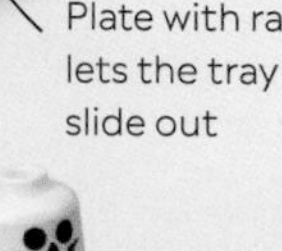

WELCOME HOME, CHARLIE AND MAYA!
THIS PARTY IS A GREAT SURPRISE!

MISSION COMPLETE

Charlie and Maya made it! It was an exciting adventure, and all their friends want to hear their stories. They faced challenges along the way, but they had fun solving them. If they get lost in the house again, they are ready for a new mission!

THAT WAS FUN!
A NEW ADVENTURE IS "STAIR-ING" ME IN THE FACE.
I COULDN'T BEAR IT WHEN THEY WERE MISSING!
WHAT WILL THE NEXT ADVENTURE BE?

GLOSSARY

Aerodynamic
If something is aerodynamic it moves easily through air because its shape creates little resistance.

Counterweight
A weight that acts as a balance to something else that has the same weight.

Current
A flow of air or water that moves in one direction.

Energy
The power needed to do something or make something go.

Envelope
The big, round part of a hot-air balloon that must be filled with air to make the balloon float.

Force
A pull or push that can move an object, change its shape, or change the way it moves.

Friction
A force that slows down a moving object when it rubs against another object.

Gravity
The natural force that pulls things toward each other. It is gravity that makes things fall to Earth.

Hover
To stay floating in the air without moving in any direction.

Kinetic energy
The energy that an object has because it is moving. The amount of kinetic energy depends partly on the object's velocity.

Material
Relating to physical objects that you can see or touch, such as wood, glass, stone, or plastic.

Mechanical energy
The energy that people and machines use to do work. It is made up of kinetic energy and stored energy.

Momentum
The tendency of a moving object to keep moving. Faster and heavier objects have more momentum than lighter and slower ones.

Optical illusion
Something that tricks your eyes and brain into seeing what is not really there.

Quantum physics
The study of things that are very, very small—even smaller than the tiny atoms that make up the universe.

Streamlined
A streamlined object has a smoother, tapering shape to move quickly and easily through air or water.

Teleportation
Moving an object directly from one place to another without crossing the space between them.

Velocity
A measure of how fast something is moving in a particular direction.

Work
In science, work is done when a force applied to something moves that thing.

MEET THE BUILDERS

KEVIN HALL

What is your favorite brick?

My favorite brick is the basic 2x4 brick, because you can create anything your imagination desires with it and it comes in almost all the LEGO® colors.

What LEGO equipment would you want to have on a mission?

The rucksack would be my equipment of choice as it would allow me to carry all my other equipment and snacks.

If you were a minifigure, which build in this book would you want to try out?

The pirate ship, because it is full of detail and can let me sail off on an adventure.

Pirate ship

Would you rather join the LEGO® pirates, knights, or party animals?

I would join the knights because I love the medieval era and love building castles.

EMILY CORL

What is your favorite brick?

I love all of the bricks. It's great to have a wide variety to build with.

If you were a minifigure, which build in this book would you want to try out?

The confetti cannon, because it starts every great party.

Would you rather join the LEGO pirates, knights, or party animals?

I would join the party animals because I love animals, and the party animals know how to have fun.

What LEGO equipment would you want to have on a mission?

I would want the swimming flippers because I love being in the water and swimming fast.

Confetti cannon

USEFUL BRICKS

All LEGO® bricks are useful, but some are more helpful than others when it comes to building on a mission! Don't worry if you don't have all of these parts. Be creative with the pieces you do have.

Small parts and small balls can cause choking if swallowed. Not for children under 3 years.

BRICK BASICS

Bricks are the basis of most LEGO builds. They come in many shapes and sizes and are named according to size.

3

2x3 brick top view

2x3 brick side view

Plates are the same as bricks, only slimmer. Three stacked plates are the same height as a standard brick.

1x2 plate

3 1x2 plates

1x2 brick

Tiles look like plates, but without any studs on top. This gives them a smooth look for more realistic builds.

2x2 round tile

1x2 tile

Slopes are any bricks with diagonal angles. They can be big, small, curved, or inverted (upside-down).

1x2 inverted slope

1x3 curved slope

COOL CONNECTORS

Bricks don't have to be stacked. Connect elements in different ways using some of these pieces.

THESE LOOK LIKE HANDY PIECES!

Any piece with a **bar** can fit onto a piece with a **clip**.

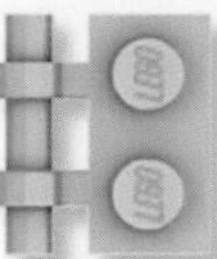

1x2 plate with handle

1x1 plate with clip

1x2 plate with bar

There are different kinds of **bricks with side studs**. They all allow you to build outward as well as upward.

1x1 brick with one side stud

1x2x2 brick with four side studs

1x2/2x2 angle plate

Jumper plates allow you to "jump" the usual grid of LEGO studs.

1x2 jumper plate

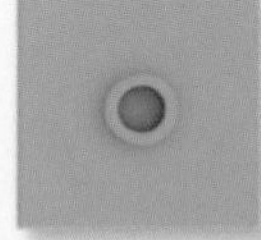

2x2 jumper plate

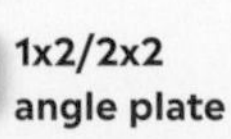

INTERESTING PIECES

Personalize your builds with some fun elements. Try adding food pieces, creatures, or anything that sparks your imagination.

Light brick

1x2 printed tile

2x2 round printed tile

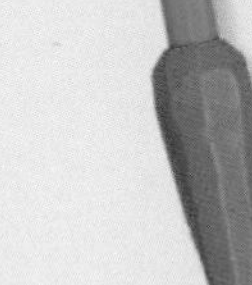
Carrot and carrot top

Cupcake piece

1x1 transparent round plate

Bat

Starfish piece

VEHICLE PARTS

Cars, trains, planes, and other things that go are helpful for getting out of trouble during an adventure. Here are some good parts for building vehicles.

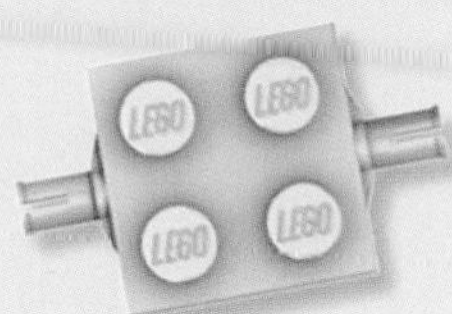
2x2 plate with pins

3x3x2 cone

Console with steering wheel

Wheel with tire

1x2 plate with ball joint

1x2x3 transparent panel

Joystick

1x2 plate with socket

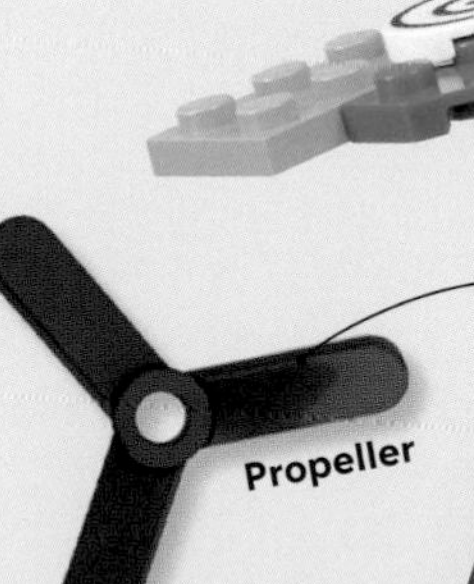
Propeller

EQUIPMENT

Useful tools and gadgets come in handy for completing any mission. Make sure to build in plenty of things to help your minifigures on their way.

LEGO string

Walkie-talkie

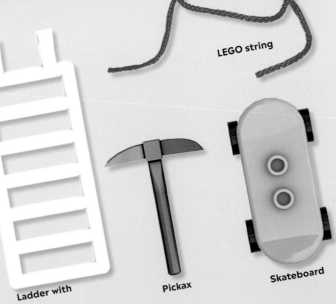

Ladder with clips

Pickax

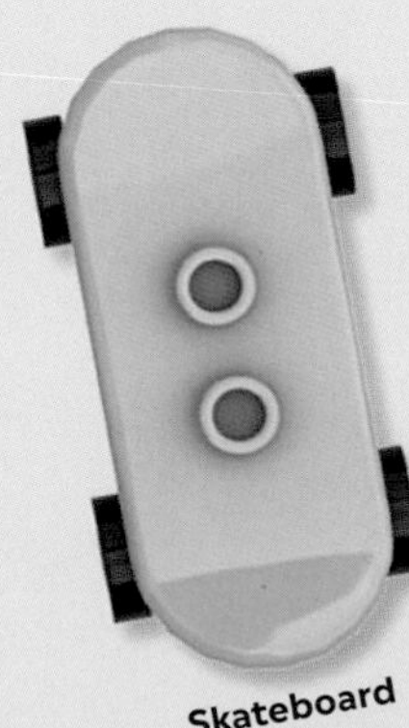
Skateboard

Flipper

I'M READY FOR A MISSION!

DK
Penguin
Random
House

Senior Editor Tori Kosara
Senior Designers Lauren Adams, Anna Formanek
Designer James McKeag
Editorial Assistant Nicole Reynolds
Senior Production Editor Jennifer Murray
Senior Production Controller Lloyd Robertson
Managing Editor Paula Regan
Managing Art Editor Jo Connor
Publishing Director Mark Searle

Models designed and created by Emily Corl and Kevin Hall
Additional models by Jason Briscoe, Stuart Crenshaw, Naomi Farr, Rod Gillies, Barney Main, and Simon Pickard
STEM consultant Ben Morgan
Photography by Gary Ombler

Dorling Kindersley would like to thank Randi Sørensen, Heidi K. Jensen, Paul Hansford, Martin Leighton Lindhardt, Charlotte Neidhardt, and Nina Koopmann at the LEGO Group. Also, at DK, Beth Davies for editorial help, Julia March for writing the glossary, Jenny Edwards for design assistance, Nicole Reynolds for additional text, and Megan Douglass for Americanizing. DK also thanks Guy Harvey, Thelma-Jane Robb, and Lisa Sodeau for design help; and Julie Ferris and Lisa Lanzarini.

First American Edition, 2021
Published in the United States by DK Publishing
1745 Broadway, 20th Floor, New York, NY 10019

23 24 25 10 9 8 7 6 5 4 3
005-321877-Oct/2021

A catalog record for this book is available from the Library of Congress.
ISBN: 978-0-7440-2865-2
978-0-7440-4343-3 (library edition)

Printed and bound in China

For the curious

www.LEGO.com
www.dk.com

MIX
Paper from
responsible sources
FSC
www.fsc.org
FSC™ C018179

This book was made with Forest Stewardship Council ™ certified paper–one small step in DK's commitment to a sustainable future. For more information go to www.dk.com/our-green-pledge

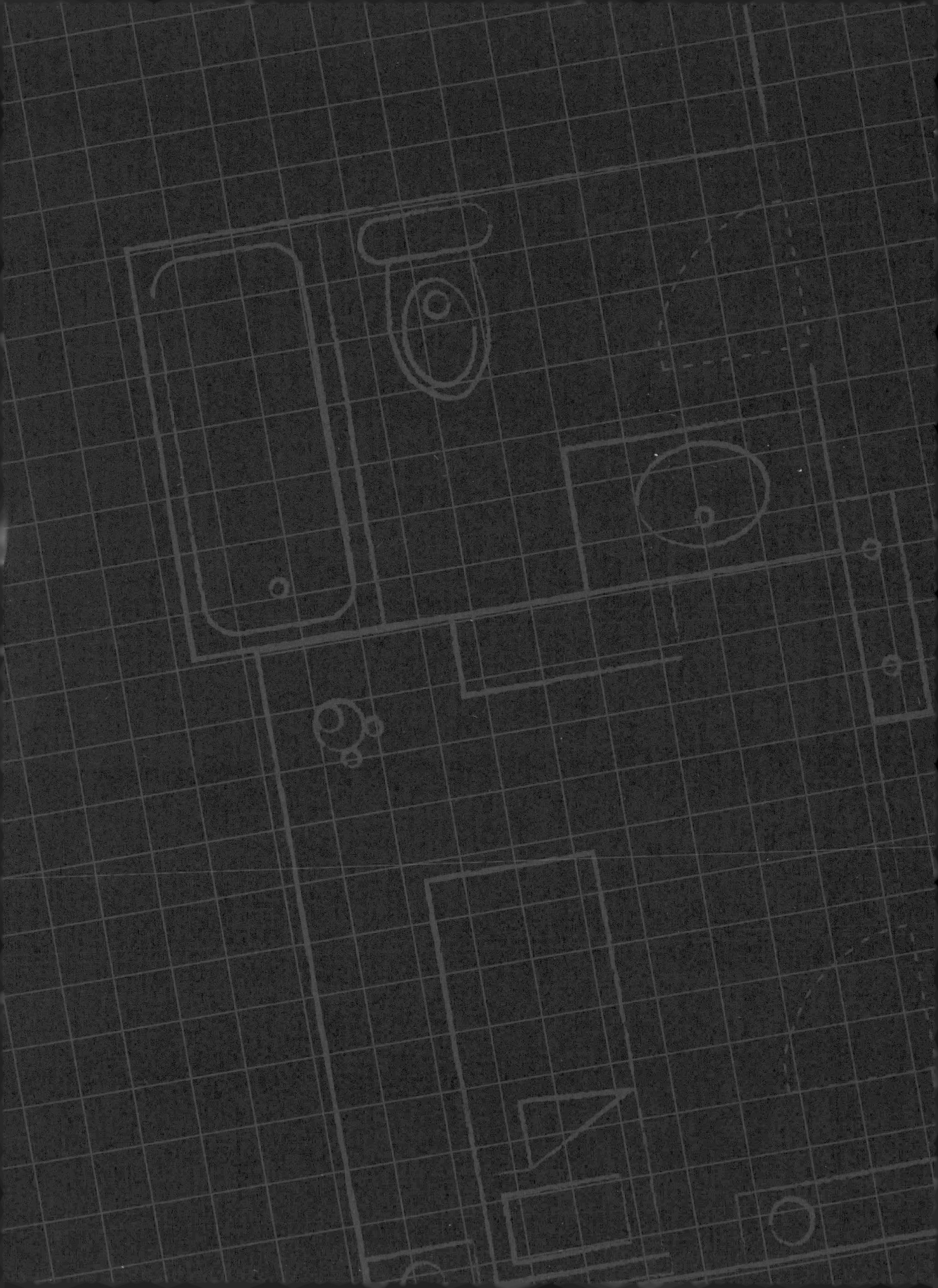